The Infected: Jim's First Day

By Joseph "Zombie" Zuko

Thank you to Josh McCullough, Kim Hill, Linda Kim and Pam Anderson for helping me edit my book.

Thank you to my Mom and Dad for always being so supportive.

Thank you to Sam for the idea to start writing this book.

Thank you to my wife Katie Zuko. She cheers me on like I am her local sports team and thank you for not letting me give up on my dreams.

Dedicated to all three of my zombie loving children.

Cover art by Paul Copeland

mailto:paulsartspace@yahoo.com

How this whole damn thing started.
A short story about Joe Zuko.

In 1997 I was a freshman in college, had a full time job and just turned nineteen. I still lived at home with my folks and they told me that if I wanted to start building credit I should go to Sears and get a credit card. I was a man now so I needed to have credit in order to buy things in the future, right? No one wants to marry a man that isn't up to his eyeballs in soul crushing debt. At least that's what I thought back then. I ran down to Sears, applied for a card and got approved for about three hundred dollars. I didn't need a Kenmore washer and dryer. I didn't need Craftsman tools. I owned a TV already and computers cost too much. I did the manliest thing I could do and bought a Playstation and the game Resident Evil 2. The game scared the poopoo out of me. I played late at night in my dark room and jumped at every scare. After that I was hooked. Zombies terrified me and I loved it. The idea that anyone can get infected and be turned into a lethal killing machine thrilled me to the bone. Grandma gets bit on the hand and now she can't be trusted. She wants to eat your face. That's really, really scary. I don't care who you are. If Grandma wants to tear out your guts and chew on them, that's scarier than sharks, chainsaws, dying in your dreams or camping with a maniac. I hope you enjoy reading my nightmare.

Table of Contents

Chapter 1

"Yes! There it goes," I roll off of my wife.

"I told you it would be worth the wait," she puts her hand up in the air for me to give it a high-five. It had been a full week since our last physical encounter, but she is right. It was worth the wait.

"To date night," the palm of my hand smacks hers. We try every week to have a date night. Even if we can't afford it we figure out some way to go out and be alone without the kids. You can't have a wrestling match in bed if you are worried that your five year old might open the door and ask, "What are you guys doing?"

She pulls our top of the line Ikea comforter up to her chest "To date night," she says as she turns to face me. Her beautiful mane of red hair has gone wild from our marital acrobatics. I wipe a little sweat from my forehead. I am not surprised. I sweat super easy. Sexy, I know.

"It is times like these I wished we smoked," I mime smoking.

"We'd look so cool. Like a couple of sexy dragons breathing fire after a night of getting busy," she copies me and pretends to smoke. We take one last fake puff and I mock blowing smoke rings.

"What time is it?" I search for my phone on the nightstand. "Oh, shit. It's nine fifteen. We gotta jet. The baby-sitter is gonna turn into a pumpkin," I pull back the covers and get out of bed.

"Five more minutes, please," she drops her face down onto her pillow and acts like she is dead.

"We gotta go. Your Mom hates staying up this late," I search for my clothes, but I can't find them in the dark. I turn on the closet light. My wife hisses. She acts like a vampire that has been hit by a sunbeam.

"Too bright! Too bright," she tosses and turns under the covers. I find my underwear and she props herself up in the bed. "A show?" she gets excited.

"You want some reverse stripping?" I ask as my hips begin to move, back and forth and side to side. I do a little drumbeat with my mouth. Boom, chi, boom, boom, chi.

"Mommy likey," she claps her hands as I slowly work my clothes back on. "Put it on," she does the drumbeat with me as I fight to pull my shirt over my head. Socks are the hard part. Have you ever tried to put your socks on and make it sexy? It is not easy, but somehow I do it. I work at getting the second sock on when I lose my balance and fall to my face.

"I'm okay," I give her a thumbs up from the floor.

I carry my sleeping two year old out the front door of my mother in law's.

"Thank you, Penny. We appreciate it," I say over my shoulder to her as I head for my wife's car.

"Thank you, Mama. I'm sorry it is so late. Say goodnight to Ganny," my wife, Karen tells our oldest Valerie.

"Thank you, Ganny. Love you," Valerie gives her about three more hugs before we go. She is a really sweet kid.

"You're welcome sweetheart," Penny's southern accent is still strong. She has lived here in the Northwest for twenty years, but she sounds like she just stepped off the porch of an old Southern plantation. She gives us a tired wave from her doorway before stepping back inside.

I hit the button on my key fob and my wife's PT Cruiser unlocks.

"Did you have fun?" Karen leads Valerie to her car seat.

"Yeah. I played computer. I had popsicles. Ganny said I could have two popsicle as long as I keep it secret," she realizes what she just said. Her secret is out. Karen and I make a silly face at her. She does not have the skills to cover up this blunder.

Karen helps her out of this mess, "How many Popsicles did you have?"

I mouth the word "One." Valerie picks up what we are doing.

"I had one popsicle. That is all," she nods her little head at us. Like she really pulled the wool over our eyes.

We get both kids into their car seats. Valerie yawns and stretches her arms out, "I am so tired."

"Close your eyes and go to sleepy, baby," Karen puts her hand over Valerie's eyes. Forcing them closed. She fakes being asleep already. Her body goes limp and she lets out some snores.

I wrestle our two-year-old, Robin, into her car seat. This is a delicate process. If she wakes up too much on the drive home or on the lay down into bed then she will wake all the way up and Karen's night is ruined. I have to be at work early so it would be up to Karen to stay awake with this little one. Her eyes stay closed but she gets a few words out.

"Where, Ganny?" she asks.

"At her house," I tell her softly.

"Where, Aler?" her little ginger head bobs around. Aler is what she calls Valerie.

"Right next to you. Go back to sleep," I click the last safety harness.

"Okay," her head drops and she is back asleep. Damn, I wish it were that easy for me. I gently close her door. We climb quietly into the front seats. I slide the key into the ignition and turn it. The PT cruiser comes alive and the radio blasts us with today's top hits. We/I forgot to turn the radio down before turning off the car. Robin wakes up with a scream. My wife looks at me like I am a dirty motherfucker.

"Oops. Sorry," I whisper to her.

There is levity in her voice, but she also means it, "You will be sorry," she looks at me with a set of classic Nic Cage crazy eyes. I put the car into reverse and pull out of Mom's driveway.

This is my family. My name is Jim.

"Sales call. Sales call! Jim, sales call one nine zero."

I snap out of my mid workday fog and pick up the phone. "Hello, this is Jim, how can I help you today?" I say that I want to help them, but I want them to go away, leave me alone, and stop bugging me. I do not care that your stupid appliance is dead.

"Oh, you need a new washer. Don't want to spend a lot. Yeah, I can help you with that." It is just another day of my life talking to people about stuff that I do not care about.

"What was that? Yes, I'm listening," I am not listening. I am thinking about home. A beer in my hand, good movie on the TV, wife and kids on the couch. That is heaven for a guy like me. Better than any vacation. Here at work is not hell; it's more like purgatory. Purgatory with John Mayer's greatest hits playing on the sound system. I have been with this company for over ten years, that is one third of my life. That is over ten Black Fridays, ten Christmases, ten years of working every weekend and missing family events. The pay is good, but this line of work can be hard on the brain. It is a "Brain Drain". That is what we call sales. Well, I am the only one that says it and I never say it out loud, but we all feel it. Tired and drained after a long day.

The customer chats my ear off. I look across the sales floor. It is a three level showroom with beautiful kitchen displays. The front of the store is all windows. They stretch floor to ceiling and look out into a busy intersection. We are located in an old part of Portland and most of the houses in this area are anywhere from sixty to a hundred years old. I get to see these large homes everyday at work. They sit only two hundred feet away from where I stand. Beautiful million dollar homes with amazing front yards and at the end of every day I go home to my crummy little apartment. My family, all four of us squeezed tightly into eight hundred square feet of living space. I have no front yard, no back yard, and no garage. We feel packed in on top of each other. I am so jealous. I can't imagine having space. A space to call my own. A little room only for me to play in.

"Mmmhmm," I mutter into the phone.

Across the street is a school for the gifted. I don't mean mutants. A school for people who either have a fully functioning brain but the body doesn't work right or the reverse. They like to eat their packed lunches on the sidewalk when it is sunny like it is today. So on one side I am wracked with jealousy wishing I had the money to afford one of those houses I see everyday and on the other side I feel blessed that I am not disabled or need to be pushed around in a wheelchair.

"Sale goes all weekend," I regurgitate.

Kitty-corner from the school is a Jiffy Lube. The guys working there are good salt of the earth types. They are always out there on the sidewalk with a sign, trying to wave down customers. So, I have that to be thankful for too. I am in an air conditioned building, never break a sweat and those poor guys are under hot cars making half as much as I do. Oh, to be a middle aged, mid income white guy at the greatest time in history. Smart enough to know that there is more out there than this, but dumb and lazy enough not to do anything about it. I get the customer's info, tell them my name a few times so they know to ask for me and try and get off the phone. It is lunchtime and lunch takes precedence over all things work related.

I hit the lunchroom. My coworker and friend, a skinny guy named Sam, sits at the table and delicately eats his homemade salad. The guy can eat anything he wants and never gains any weight, but he still eats salad. Motherfucker. He sports the thickest rimmed glasses you have ever seen. Like he wants to look like a nerd. Not the cool nerds that work at Apple or some Internet startup company. He looks like a caricature of a nerd.

"It's slow out there today, man," I drop my lunch bag on the table and take a seat. "Haven't sold jack."

"I had a laydown on a kitchen package this morning," Sam gloats. "Over ten thou' going out this month." Sam had a crazy knack for walking into easy sick deals where the customer is ready to buy and he makes tons of money. He is the number one guy at our store. I hate him, but he makes me laugh so his lucky ass gets to be my best friend. He pulls his feet out from under the table. "Check out the new kicks." My eyes drop down to look at his very shiny new shoes.

"Fancy," I tell him. He is so proud of his footwear. I never make fun. Not ever. No matter how silly I think it is for a man to buy so many new shoes. I don't say anything. "How much did they set you back?" the number will shock me. It always does.

"I got them on sale. Four ninety-nine," he nods his head.

"Wow. What a deal," I nod my head too and make sure there is no sarcasm in my voice at all. They look like something Clark Griswold wore in *National Lampoon's European Vacation*. The shoes have sharp angles and useless straps, but he loves them.

"Yeah, my guy can totally hook you up if you ever want to dip into the luxury shoe game," he bites the last of his low fat salad.

"Okay. Maybe. I'll talk with Karen. See if it's in the budget," I smile at him, but there is no way in hell Karen would ever let me have shoes that cost more than three lap dances.

The phone on the wall chimes. "Sam, you have a customer waiting down on the sales floor."

He gets up, puts his plate in the dishwasher, "Back to the salt mine."

"Go sell another ten you bastard," we fist bump. I am not a fan of this form of nonverbal communication. I prefer the high five. I pride myself on giving the best high fives. The power comes from the elbow and a good one will leave your palm stinging. He actually walks different when he has a new set of shoes. If he spent half the amount he does on new shoes he could get eye surgery and not have to wear those nerd glasses.

I crack open my lunch bag. The wife was nice enough to pack it for me this morning. Even with the radio mishap last night she still got up early to make it for me. I have been trying to lose weight so it is all healthy, organic and fresh. I hate it, but I am down over twenty pounds. You can't argue with results. The food tastes good but I don't like to admit it. There is something to be said about eating bad foods; it is very satisfying to finish off three thousand calories in one really sloppy cheeseburger. I can't put my finger on what it is but it most likely has to do with the salt and fat. I am no scientist. Karen packed me a wonderful chicken salad wrap today. I can truly say my wife is the best. She is a stay-at-home mom with our two beautiful, sweet kids.

My cell says I got a text. "drink water" It's her. She knows that I forget to drink water throughout my workday. I text her back "will do, Luv u".

Two years ago I got a wake up call. I was topping over two ten. I was brewing my own beer and drinking six a night. I am a sucker and a chump for India Pale Ale's. Karen said I needed to stop and I had to go to the doctor for a checkup. I was in high school when I had my last checkup. I found out I had crazy high cholesterol. It runs in the family. So that year for Christmas Karen bought me a month of Krav Maga classes. Here honey, here's a present, lose weight you chubby bastard. I go and fall in love with it. Almost two years in now and I have five colorful belts hanging on the wall.

To get one of those belts you have to go through hell. It is a four-hour nonstop physical test. You have to show the instructors everything you learned over the last three months. Plus you get to do a ton of sparring. You fight people of different levels. Some are brand new and it is easy. One night I sparred with a guy that was one level away from black belt. He kicked my ass all over the mat. When you get to the end of a test you really feel like you earned it. The class itself is a lot of cardio but you do learn how to kick ass on the street. Now my weight and cholesterol are finally under control. My shoulder, chest to belly ratio is at a place where I feel comfortable with my shirt off. I take one bite of my organic fresh chicken salad wrap and the phone on the wall chimes.

"Jim, please see the manager."

Bill has been my manager for five years now. He does this almost everyday. He knows I am at lunch but he calls me down to his office to bullshit with me. He is the best manager I have ever had. He sits back in his office all day and only comes out to tell jokes. So I pack up my lunch.

The lunchroom is on the second floor of my store. As I leave the room I step out onto the upper sales floor. It is all mattresses and TVs. I pass by a four thousand dollar mattress and I so want to go to sleep. I share the bed with Karen and Robin. It is a rough nights sleep on an old queen mattress when a two year old keeps kicking you in the back. I cross the floor and pass by one of the most beautiful things I have ever seen. It is an amazing seventy-inch super, ultra high definition TV. I want one so bad, but it does not make a lot of sense to have one that big if you can only sit five feet from it. I am almost out of the department when our warehouse man waves me down. His name is Devon. He is a man, technically, but really he is a kid. He is twenty, I think. He gives me a heavy nod when I make eye contact with him. His head bobs up and down like a silly toy from a foreign country.

"Dude, I saw a crazy one last night," he always calls me "Dude." He is not a surfer or a skater, but he loves the word dude.

"Really? What was it?" I nod my head to match his nod. He is talking about a horror movie. He is always talking about a horror movie. I don't/can't watch them anymore. I get the worst nightmares. Plus my kids are always up.

"Dude, this killer was after this girl. He like, killed her parents ten years ago and now he was back to finish the job," Devon gets crazy eyes every time he says the word killer. "You will never guess how he kills people," he shakes his head at me. This is the part where I get to guess how the killer kills them.

"Was it a gun?" I don't really try anymore. I never get it right.

"No, dude. He would suffocate them with a plastic bag and then take their skin off with like a nasty old blade. It was so good, dude.

I was so scared. It's a crazy Russian movie I downloaded," he nods his head at me and I never know what to say.

"Cool. I gotta get to Bill's office. Talk to you later," I head down for the stairway.

My thighs kill me as I walk down the steps. I threw a lot of kicks at the last Krav Maga class. On the way down I run into Tracy, our front desk phone operator. She is my age and distractingly pretty.

"Did I show you the photo?" it is going to be about her kids, kind of. I made the mistake of becoming her Facebook friend and every goddamn post is about her kids, kind of. I smile big at her and shake my head.

"Nope. Haven't seen them," I prepare myself for her photos. She pulls her phone from her pocket. Her photos are always the same kind of funny thing where her kids are in them, but the photo is her looking super sexy. Why is this sexy lady in this child's photo? She flashes me her phone.

"Look at this," she says. Acting very innocent. It is a photo of her right out of the shower with nothing but a towel clinging to her shapely body and an eight-year-old making a funny face in the background.

"Boy, that is a cute kid."

"Isn't he? I look horrible. Don't look at me," she fishes for a compliment. This has been happening more and more since she left her weirdo husband.

"No, you look...amazing. Better than I do straight out of the shower," what else can I say? She is the one that called me down to Bill's office and I bet she planned this whole rendezvous.

"Thank you. You are so sweet," she brushes my arm with her hand. I pretend like it didn't happen.

"Okay, Bill needs me," I turn and head down the stairs.

I knock at Bill's open door. I know what three jokes are coming. He is going to tease me about Krav Maga. He calls it "Teal Macaw". It is not a clever joke but he loves it. Then he will say I am wasting my time working out. He never works out and he has had a better life than me. Then he will tease me about my numbers, me versus Sam. Bill sits there at his desk. He is always smiling. He points at a bruise on my wrist.

"Is that from Teal Macaw?" joke number one out of the way.

"Yeah, I caught an elbow to the wrist in class. Hurt like hell."

"Why do you waste your time with working out? It is hours a week you could be having way more fun. I never workout and I definitely have more fun than you," joke two right on schedule. I look at Bill's big belly, but I do not say anything. Bill picks up a print out of the store's numbers.

"Boy, Sam is killing you again this month. If I could make a clone of that guy I'd get all my bonuses," joke three, the trifecta. Now we can start our normal conversation.

BOOM! My fillings shake as the ground moves under my feet. I feel intense heat from a massive explosion outside.

Chapter 2

I almost shit my pants. Seconds after the explosion there is a loud crash. I step from Bill's office doorway and onto the sales floor. I drop my lunch bag. My jaw drops too. All of the windows facing the Jiffy Lube are blown out. Shattered glass covers all of the appliances. The front row of washers has caught fire. An old beat up van has crashed through the wall. Its front end rests on a knocked over stacked laundry set. The van is on fire too. Sam cowers behind the dishwasher display. His customer bleeds out on the floor. She has a large jagged chunk of metal sticking out of her throat. The Jiffy Lube is engulfed in flames. I step farther out onto the floor. My eyes blink quickly trying to process what I see. A helicopter has crash-landed on the Jiffy Lube.

Boom!

Something else inside the Jiffy Lube explodes. I duck behind the dishwasher display next to Sam. He has a slice running jagged down his cheekbones. Blood cascades down onto his dress shirt. Sam pulls off his glasses. The lenses are scratched to hell. If it weren't for his astigmatism he would be blind right now. Thank God for those nerd glasses. Boom! Another explosion rocks the building.

"What the fuck happened?" Sam grabs at me. He is talking louder than normal. A face full of explosion must have messed with his hearing. I look over the dishwashers. The tail end of the helicopter reads Providence Hospital. That hospital is only a mile away.

"It must have had engine problems. Oh God! All those guys are dead."

18

Sam sticks his fingers in his ears. He works to get his hearing back.

"Should I lock the doors?" yells Bill.

"What's the point? We don't have a wall right now." I yell back. Why am I yelling? I am not mad at Bill. My hands shake and my heart beats hard enough that I can feel my pulse on my forehead. Goddamn this is the most exciting thing I have ever seen. I look around the floor and no one else is hurt. Tracy was over at her desk on the other side of the building. She has come around her desk to get a better look at the action. The poor girl has peed her pants. The front of her khakis are soaked. I look away. I don't want her to know that I saw it. I don't blame her. I am about to unload in the back of my slacks.

I pull my cell out and dial 911. The phone rings and rings. No answer. I hang up and try again. The Jiffy Lube burns, all that oil, it looks like a photo from the Gulf War. Black smoke fills the sky and lays down a thick fog on the ground around it. Some blood has got onto one of Sam's new shoes. He quickly rubs the blood off his leather footwear and it gets all over his hand. He shows me the blood on his hand. Like I need to clean it for him. That is when he notices his customer on the ground. The blood on his shoe came from her.

"Linda, are you okay?!" he shakes her body.

"I don't think she's okay!" I give up on my phone and put it in my pocket.

"She's dead," Sam loses it. "She's DEAD! Oh, SHIT!" his voice cracks. He looks up at me. I nod.

"Yeah Sam. No one's answering at 911. Bill, get him up and get him some water."

Bill snaps to. I get up and run over to the closest fire extinguisher. My nerves are so shot it takes me a full minute to read the instructions. It has only two steps but it is like I have never read English before. The van's engine runs like the driver has his foot all the way to the floor. Between it and the other fires going on, this place is filling up with smoke quickly. I finally master the art of the extinguisher and sprint to the closest flame. I have always wanted to do this. Shoot an extinguisher on a flame, I mean. It always looked so cool on TV. Behind me Devon has emerged with his own fire retardant device and the two of us go to work.

Even with all of the excitement and tragedy going on I am very aware of how sexually charged this act is. Hear me out. The flame burns so bright, so hot and the only thing that can quench its desire and put the flame to rest is two young men shooting it with white foam. I get it. I am the gross one. If Devon and I were being filmed in slow-mo with eighties butt-rock blasting, you would see what I mean. We finish putting the fires out on the appliances when our extinguishers run out of juice. The van continues to burn in the corner of the store. I look around for the next red can when the sprinklers go off. We are doused with water. These sprinklers are not messing around. In a matter of seconds I am completely soaked. The van's fire has gone out. That's good, I guess. Devon and I toss our cans to the ground. Tracy's accident has been washed away as well. I survey the showroom. The owner is going to be pissed. All of these appliances, TV's and beds are ruined. I guess that's what insurance is for.

"This is some crazy shit, Dude."

"Yes, Devon. This is some crazy shit. Dude," I wipe the water away from my eyes.

I take a look around outside. All of the students from the school for the gifted are on the sidewalk watching Jiffy Lube burn to the ground. I head over to the front door and pop it open.

"Is everyone okay?!" I yell across the street. One of the female instructors shouts back.

"We're good! I can't get 911 on the phone. Sprinklers went off?" she asks with a smirk.

"Yeah, we're all soaked. I couldn't reach them either. We have someone that got...hurt here," I don't want any of the students to get upset so I lie. "Keep calling them! I'm gonna check on the other neighbors."

She gives me a thumb up and puts her phone to her ear. On the other side of our building is an adult video store with live shows in the back. Karen and I used to go to strip clubs when we were in our twenties. It was a lot of fun to bring her because women get a lot of attention at those places. Afterwards we would go home and, well…it was always fun. I have always wanted to go into that store but never had a good enough reason. I turn back into my showroom and see a miracle. Linda, Sam's customer, is back on her feet and walking around.

"Miss? You should lay back...," my words slow down as Linda turns to face me. Her eyes have filled with blood. So full that they look purple. She stands there looking around and she is not breathing. That's weird. You wouldn't think you would notice a little thing like that but seeing a human stand upright staring at you, your brain says, "That crazy bitch ain't breathing!"

"Linda?" Sam says in shock. His glasses look like fishbowls; they are so full of water. Linda's head whips around to face him. She sprints right for him! In a flash she has him on the floor. Sam clutches her by the shoulders. Her teeth snap at his face!

"Holy fuck!" I yell it from across the sales floor. Ten years I have been on this floor and it is the first time I have ever cursed out loud.

I run to Sam's aid. The woman has gone nuts. The hunk of metal in her neck must be incredibly painful to make her act this way. I grab her shoulder.

"Hey lady, knock it off," she turns her head towards me and the wound in her neck opens up. That chunk of metal goes deep into her. She should not even be moving. What is going on? She snaps her teeth at my hand and I pull it back right before she takes a finger off.

"What's your problem, lady?!"

"Get her off me!" Sam desperately fights against her. For the last two years I have been trying to get Sam to come to Krav Maga class with me and his answer was always, "I'd never use it." Well right now he could use it. Linda only weighs one twenty and has a major neck wound. I could get her off me in two seconds. Sam acts like she is a sumo wrestler. I grab Linda and toss her to the ground. Her head smacks against the wet carpet. It doesn't faze her. She rolls over and grabs for my leg. I step back so she can't reach me.

"Bill, we gotta get this lady out of here. She's crazy!" Linda slowly gets up.

"Lady, if you don't stop acting nuts, I'm gonna have to put you on your ass!"

I take a fighting stance out of habit. I did not even think about it. As soon as she moves for me, my hands are up and ready. She leaps, arms out, teeth snapping. So I throw a front kick, hard, right into her chest. Her ribs break on impact. She hits the ground and again she starts to get back to her feet!

My work crew watches me fight this tiny lady and I look like a wimp. Like my kicks are for shit but I know that was a hard one. She should not be able to breathe. That is when I notice it again. She is still not breathing. How can that be? She makes a lot of noise with her mouth but she is not really breathing. I am hyperventilating over here.

"Look!" Bill points across the street at the Jiffy Lube. A dark figure moves among the flames. It steps out of the wreckage. Its skin drips off of its body as it slowly shuffles out of the flames. One of its arms falls to the burning asphalt. It is still on fire. I mean the person's body is still on fire. It continues to burn as it walks out onto the street.

"WHAT THE FUCK!?!" I am sure we all said it.

My attention is back on Linda. There she is, arms out, eyes purple, teeth bared, making me look like a punk. That is it. No more mister nice sales guy. I throw a kick and make contact with her knee. The joint folds backwards. As she stumbles forward I hit her in the jaw with my elbow, breaking it badly. She falls to her side. This time I got her. TKO in the first round! I look over at everyone in my store. I feel like Rocky and I just laid out Apollo Creed. My coworkers are not even looking at me.

I follow their eyes out to the street. Six more burnt black bodies, are climbing out of the fire. They all look like the Human Torch. The oil at the Jiffy Lube makes their bodies burn bright. Two of them walk over to the school. They look more like demon fire creatures than humans. They look bizarre, because I am used to seeing a human on fire move very quickly. It is normally a stuntman that darts off screen after only a few seconds of being set ablaze. These guys walk with purpose. Not slow. Methodical would be the best way to describe it. Screams come from the gifted. A few of the should-be-corpses walk towards the adult store. The last couple walks right for our open windows.

Out of the corner of my eye I see that Linda is back on her feet. Man, this girl can take a beating. I am in shock. Her jaw is on her face but it hangs at an extreme angle. I look back out the window. More shock. I wish there was another saying for the level above, "What the fuck?!" but my brain is shutting down. Game over! These "people" feel no pain and oxygen is not a priority.

Clearly I never woke up this morning. This is a sick dream my overworked brain has created. I am waiting for my alarm clock to go off. Any minute now I should be waking up. Nope. Linda tries to take another piece off of me. She wobbles towards me. Her broken knee makes it hard for her to stand up straight. Her jaw snaps back into place when she tries to bite.

"Everyone upstairs!"

"Dude!" I look over at Devon as he tosses me a fire extinguisher. I catch it and swing

it in one move. I hold it by the hose and nail
Linda right in the face. DONG! It sends her
backwards over a portable dishwasher. The
water stops dumping on us the second she hits
the floor. I run my hand through my hair and
wipe a gallon of water off my face. None of my
coworkers have taken a step. Their eyes stay
focused on the two fire monsters that have
entered our store. It is a bad time for the
sprinklers to stop pouring water.

They walk right for me. Linda has gotten
back to her feet again. The fire monsters
bodies fall apart the closer they get to me.
One of their arms drops off and lands in a
basket full of towels we use to show off the
capacity of the new washers.

"Upstairs now!" I toss the extinguisher
at them and it knocks one of them to the
ground. I make for the stairs and push Sam to
move. The five of us head for the employee
only stairwell. They push open the fire door
to the stairs. It is made out of solid steel.
I am the last one through the door and I slip
the bolt lock into place behind me. The steps
are soaking wet and slick as hell. My brain
scrambles to figure out what the hell is going
on. How is this possible?! Is this happening
everywhere?! What about Karen and the kids?!

The top floor of our building is a
warehouse. It's where we keep refrigerators,
washers, dryers and beds. I am the last
through the door and I point to Devon.

"Help me with this!" I grab a
refrigerator box. We tip it over so it falls
against the closed door. Backing away from the
overturned box, we hear the sounds of fists
hitting the steel door on the floor below.

"They're trying to get in," I mutter
under my breath. I fish my phone from my

pocket. I speed dial my wife. When I got this smartphone the sales guy talked me into the eighty-dollar waterproof case. He said most people use their phones when they are taking a dump. Mine never slipped down between my legs and into the water, but right now I am thankful I got the heavy-duty case. I am totally soaked and it still works. She answers in two rings.

"Hello," she says sweetly. I can tell from her voice she is fine, but I still ask.

"Karen! Are you and the kids okay?!"

"Yeah? What's up?" she has no idea.

"Turn on the news!" I have a hard time keeping calm.

"What's happened?" I hear the TV fire up. As she does that, I jog over to one of the windows that gives us access to the roof above the showroom. I crack it open.

"Holy shit! Is this for real? What happened to these people?"

"What does it say?" I climb out the window and head for the edge of the building. Sam and Devon follow after me onto the roof.

"It says...people that were dead are getting up and if they bite you...I don't know? There is also something about an infection spreading from the hospitals. It must be a prank?" her voice shakes.

"Baby, lock the front and back door. Try and put something heavy in front of them," I hear our toddler trying to get her attention.

"Baby, be quiet Daddy's trying to tell me something!" Karen's voice says it all. She is more than panicked. She has never yelled at the kids like that before. Robin cries in the background.

"Karen? Lock the doors!"

The three of us have made it to the edge of the building and it is chaos down on the streets of Portland. Two of the burnt guys have smashed their way into the school and the others have broken down the doors at the adult store. Both buildings are now on fire. Screams fill the air. An ambulance hauls ass down the street. It swerves all over the road and bounces from one parked car to the next. It hits a curb and then a telephone pole. The sirens keep going as smoke pours out of the engine block. Something is tearing the driver apart!

"Baby, lock down the apartment. Keep the lights off. Don't let anyone in. Don't let them know you're there. Get the kids dressed. Then pack up some food and stay in the bedroom. Get the gun, it's in the closet. I love you and the girls. I'm coming home soon."

"We love you! Hurry!"

I don't want to hang up but I need to save my battery. I turn off my phone and put it back into my slacks. I feel the car keys in my pocket. Thank God. Sometimes I leave them in my desk. My apartment is over ten miles from here, across the river, and in the state of Washington. If this is happening everywhere the roads will be gridlocked. I am going to have to walk home. Walk ten miles and over a river to get to my girls while the world is losing its mind. First things first, I have to figure a way off this roof.

Chapter 3

We climb back into the warehouse. There is a stack of flat panel TVs close to the window we climbed out of. I pull out my Swiss Army knife and cut the box open. I get the TV out and prop it up against the wall near a power plug.

"Grab an antenna."

Devon picks up a box from a stack of accessories and pulls out an antenna. He hands it to me and I screw the cord into the back of the TV. I hand the remote over to Bill who pops the batteries out of the wrapping and drops them into the remote. He hits the power button, tells the TV to skip the setup option, clicks it over to the antenna connection and dials in our local channel eight.

"...reports stream in from all over the Northwest. There is a deadly infection spreading across the Portland and Vancouver metro area. People that were reported dead are coming back to life. I am having a hard time believing this myself folks, but I have seen the footage. All of the reports we have tell us that once a person's heart has stopped, within minutes they will come back...and every report we have received is very clear on this. After they come back they feed on human flesh. You heard me correctly, they feed on human flesh. I warn you the footage you are about to see is very graphic."

The news cuts to footage of a cameraman under attack. He uses the camera as a weapon and smashes the lens into the face of an infected man. The five of us flinch with every impact. Our stomachs turn as we watch this horrifying scene. Most of the skin is gone from its face and an eyeball hangs from its socket. The monster is relentless, it scratches and claws, teeth bared and snapping. It looks just like Linda downstairs. The camera's microphone distorts and peaks from the screams. The camera falls to the ground. It lands on its side. The young cameraman lies on his back fighting the infected human. The monster overpowers him and tears into his flesh. It bites down on his face, then his neck, and his forearm. Whatever gets close to its mouth is bit and torn from the young man's body. He succumbs to the attack and goes limp.

"This is disgusting! How can they show this on TV?" Tracy cries and tears trickle down her cheeks. My hands shake as adrenaline pumps through my body. My armpits sweat and I think I am going to puke. I look over to Sam and his face is white. Bill pukes. Even the super horror movie fan, Devon, can't look at the TV anymore.

The monster takes a few more bites then stops, lets go of its victim, stands up and walks out of camera frame. The cameraman's body pumps blood onto the ground. Within a minute the cameraman's body moves again. It sits up, gets to its feet and shuffles off. The footage stops and cuts back to the news anchor.

"Early reports are indicating that the hospitals were hit first and have been overrun. The police are outmanned and the infection is spreading fast. As you saw in the footage, once you have been bitten, or if you die, you will come back as one of them. The authorities request that you stay in your hom..." From the TV we hear a loud explosion and then the TV goes to static.

"What do we do?" Sam whispers.

I turn away from the TV and head back out the window onto the roof. I look down at the streets and it is carnage. Blood covers the windows inside the school and one by one newly infected shuffle out of the building. The gifted already had a hard time getting around when they were alive. Now it will take them forever to get anywhere. The ones that had spent their lives in a wheelchair are crawling out onto the sidewalk. It is a very messed up thing to see a dead disabled kid, covered with blood and guts, pull itself around on the ground.

It is a busy intersection and cars are flying up and down it. One of the infected steps out into oncoming traffic. A minivan slams on its brakes but it is too late. The infected body destroys the hood and is upended, shattering the windshield. The driver pulls into the next lane and hits a truck head on. The sound of crushing metal, glass and bones breaking is worse than anything you hear in the movies. The vehicles twist and spin around each other. Both cars come to a screeching halt. The driver is laid out on the horn. Gore covers both cars. Everything that makes us human splayed out on the hoods.

Seconds later, cars coming from both directions crash into the wreck. The infected swarm the cars and smash in the windows. I can hear women and children crying from their cars. People try to help, but they are overtaken and torn to pieces.

A topless woman from the adult store runs screaming into the street. She has been bit on her legs and back. A group of half-naked women follow her. The fire from the Jiffy Lube has spread to the trees that separate it from a million dollar home. A man stands in his front yard with a garden hose and tries to put out the fire. Everyone joins me at the edge of the roof.

"Look," I point to the man.

"He has no idea what's happening," Sam states the obvious.

We watch as the topless woman runs right for him. He drops his hose and she runs into his arms. It is like he can only see her boobs and not the infected chasing after her. We can't hear what he is saying to her, but it looks like he is telling her to calm down. The other girls are in his yard now. He holds up his hand and tells them to stop. The topless girl lets go of him and runs for his front door. The group is on him and tears him to the ground.

The people that were bitten in their cars have changed and now join the other infected out in the street. It is a small horde already and it has only been ten minutes since the helicopter hit the Jiffy Lube.

We hear sirens from a police car, it pulls onto the street and stops next to the man getting torn apart on his front yard. Two cops get out of the car and draw their weapons. They scream for the infected to stop and put their hands into the air. They leave the dead man on the grass and run right at the two officers. They open fire and empty both of their clips in seconds. Two of the girls are hit and sent to the ground. The officers are aiming for the chest, like they are trained to do, but it does not stop the infected. The man on the driver's side is attacked. The second officer changes his clip as he runs around the front of the car to help his partner. The officer under attack throws punches and kicks, trying to keep the women off him, but they keep coming. The two women on the ground get up. This time he puts a few rounds into their heads and they fall to the ground. Dead. Really dead.

The man lying on the grass has turned and he gets to his feet and runs for the officers. Again the cop fires at the head and the newly turned body fall to the street. The other officer has been bitten a few times now, but finally gets off a few rounds and shoots the last of the ladies in the head. He is hurt bad and his partner helps him to his feet. They climb back into their squad car and hit the gas. The car backs down the street leaving a trail of smoke behind them.

A red Volvo skids to a stop and runs over three infected. It high centers on the corpses, its tires spinning in the air. The driver gets out and runs to the back door, she gets her two-year-old from its car seat. She takes the baby and sprints away from us. She turns a corner. We can't see her anymore but we can hear her screams. My hand covers my mouth, the mental picture making me gag. All around us we hear screams. Breaking glass. More screams.

A big truck scoots quickly down the street. Thick metal rails hold its cargo into place. Its cargo, thirty plus aluminum tanks, rattle around in its open truck bed. On the side of the vehicle is a sign that reads "flammable." As it enters the intersection it is t-boned by another fast moving vehicle. The big truck is set off course and heads straight for the burning Jiffy Lube. The truck explodes seconds after it enters the flaming structure. The heat from this explosion almost melts my eyebrows. I duck down below the edge of the building.

"We have to get out of here!" I can't watch any more carnage below. The group ducks down with me.

"How do we get down? There's no fire escape," Sam sounds defeated already. One of the tanks from the back of the big truck explodes and shoots high into the air. The damn thing lands dead center of the roof we are standing on. We all drop to the ground and cower for our lives. It begins to burn the roof right away.

"Oh good. That's what we needed," I say sarcastically. I pop up and run across the roof and look at the back of the building. Our company sits next to an animal hospital and we also share the same parking lot. I look down and there is a van parked right next to our building. Its roof sits around twenty feet below us. Sam is right behind me.

"We jump."

"It's too far! We'll break our legs," Sam shakes his head. He is right. We will not make the jump. My car is parked only a hundred feet away, on the street behind the building. Right now I do not see any of those things back here. Yet.

I look back at the tank that is setting the whole roof on fire. "It's better than burning to death. Don't worry. I have an idea!" I climb back into the warehouse, Sam is right behind me. The rest of the group follows behind him.

"Guys we have to jump," I say with conviction.

"We can't jump from here!" squawks Bill.

"We don't have a lot of options and we have to move fast. There aren't any of them at the back of the building right now. Help me with this?" I walk over to a large stack of twin-sized mattresses; grab one off the stack and head back for the open window. Devon and Sam grab one each and follow me onto the roof. Bill and Tracy grab one together. I guess they are going to go along with this. God, I hope it works. I stand at the edge of the building. Boom! Boom! Boom! Tanks explode one after another. Each one lands in a different spot. It only adds to the chaos. More buildings are burning down. The cars closest to the Jiffy Lube are all set ablaze. Another tank explodes and lands on our roof. It is only ten feet from where we are standing. We drop to the ground and duck behind our mattresses for cover. The heat coming off it is intense. It is so hot that the plastic bag that incases the mattress has begun to melt and shrink.

"Goddamn that was close!" I fight to get back up, "Sam, grab the end of this."

Sam lets go of his mattress and picks up the end of mine. Almost half of the roof is on fire. We lift the mattress over the edge and aim for the top of the van in the parking lot.

"Ready?" I ask. Sam nods. "Drop it." We both let go and the mattress hits the top of the van perfectly. A sigh of relief...then the vans alarm goes off.

"SHIT! Lets move!" We drop the other three mattresses on top of the van as fast as we can. The fire creeps closer and closer to us. One tank after another blows apart and sends its aluminum torpedo flying into the air. "I'll go first," I throw my leg over the side of the building. I hate heights! I really, really hate heights. I am not a fan of climbing up a six-foot ladder. That is how much I hate heights. I pivot on my butt and bring my other leg over the side. I take a deep breath. I want to close my eyes but I know that is a really bad idea. I push off and try to land on my back. I fall ten feet and land hard on the stack of mattresses. I cave the top of the van in when I land. I do a quick body check and nothing has broken.

"You okay?!" Sam yells down to me.

"I'm fine," I sit up and climb down onto the hood and drop to the pavement. They send Tracy over next and she lands it perfectly. She climbs off and joins me in the parking lot.

"Hurry up!" I yell up at them. Sam goes next, then Devon. The van's alarm blasts.

"Linda?" Sam pulls at my shoulder. I turn and see her stumble out of the backdoor of our building. That demon woman has spotted us and runs as fast as she can with a busted knee. Not too far behind her is a group of infected kids from the school. They are on the other side of the parking lot and moving fast in this direction.

"Bill, jump!" He sits on the edge of the building and shakes his head.

"Stop thinking and jump!" shouts Sam.

"I can't!!"

"They're coming! We have to move!" I yell up at him. I have my keys in my hands ready to go. More of them creep around the side of the building. They file into our parking lot.

"FUCK IT!" Bill lets go of the building. His body twists in the air. He jumped too far. He is not going to land right. Goddamn it. Bill slams down on the edge of the mattresses, falls off immediately and lands hard. He puts his hands out to break his fall and both wrists snap in the wrong direction. He lands face first on the asphalt. I roll him over to his back. His nose is broken, his lips are cut and two front teeth are knocked out. He is out cold.

"Sam, grab him." We grab Bill by his arms and drag him towards the street. His hands flop around as we pull him by his forearms. The bones grind on each other inside his wrist. Linda leads the pack of infected over the fence that separates the two parking lots. Bill's body is too heavy and they gain on us with every step. I click the unlock button on my key fob, Devon and Tracy climb into the back seat. We get Bill to the street, but the infected are right behind us. There is no time to pick up his body and force it into the back of my car. They are too close. This shit can't be happening. I lock eyes with Sam. He is thinking it too. I close my eyes in despair and let go of Bill. Sam lets go as well and within seconds Linda is on him. She's quickly joined by the other infected. When her first bite cuts into his skin it wakes him up. Bill howls like an animal. His body turns over and he looks up at me. His eyes are like an abandoned child. Hurting, disbelieving, how could I possibly leave him for dead? I pop open the door to my car as Sam runs around to the passenger's side. Bill reaches out for me to save him. His hand flops around on the broken joint.

"DON'T LEAVE!!"

"WE HAVE TO HELP HIM!" Devon wails from the back seat.

"WE CAN'T!" I turn back and look at Bill. "I'M SORRY!" my throat tightens. Tears well up in my eyes. I slam my door shut, force the key into the ignition and start the car. I could not save him. Bill fights but it is too late. They pile on top of him and peel the meat from his big belly.

"PLEASE, PLEASE, PLEASE!!! HELP ME!!!"

I put the car into gear and hit the gas. The tires screech as I make a U-turn. We circle around Bill. The terror and fear in his eyes I know will haunt me for the rest of my life. Hot tears make it hard to see. I am wracked with guilt. Bill was not just my manager, he was a friend. I loved the man and I left him to die.

"What are we going to do?" Sam whispers.

"I have to get home," I can barely get the words out over the large gulps of air I am taking in. I am not a religious man but I am praying for my family. Over and over I repeat in my head. "Please let them be safe. Please let them be safe." I turn onto the road and head for home.

Chapter 4

I hammer through the gears in my car, a mid two thousands Mitsubishi Lancer. I try my best to get my emotions under control. My hands shake uncontrollably. I grip the wheel tighter to get them steady. My eyes sting. I look in the rearview mirror; they're bloodshot and wild. My breathing is erratic. I have what my wife calls the snubs. That is when a child is so upset, that they cry so hard they take in large breaths and then short breathes. I have the snubs bad.

I have never seen a human die before. Never witnessed anything like this. I am in full-blown shock. I am covered in sweat. My skin feels cold and sticky. I rub my eyes. Looking at my passengers, I don't have to ask; I know they feel the same. We will mourn Bill later, now I have to focus on the road.

I am only blocks away from my store and I have already seen cars blow through stop signs, crash into each other, run over and destroy pedestrians on the sidewalk. One car launched itself through an intersection, lost control and blasted its way through someone's garage door. We are passing over a major highway, Portland calls it Highway 84. It looks like a concrete corridor cut into the earth. It runs from one side of Portland to the other. It's the main road to travel East or West. It has eight-foot brick walls that line the highway. If you are down in it, you are stuck. Only the on and off-ramps can let you out. I take a quick glance down at the gridlock nightmare. Cars have forced themselves into the small median, pinned between the concrete divider and the cars in the fast lane. Vehicles are on fire. The lights of a police squad car and a fire truck flash in the distance. Gunshots ring out down there in the trench. The report on TV sounded like the areas around the hospitals will be heavy with the infected. Right now those officers are only a hundred yards away from Providence.

I am almost to an intersection when a logging truck blows the red light. I jam on my brakes, the tires skid and the car slides to a stop just in time. My front bumper is clipped and torn off. I hear tires screech behind us. I sink down in my seat. My eyes catch a glimpse of something big in my rear view mirror. It is a big Dodge truck barreling right for us. I brace for impact.

SMASH! It destroys my trunk and folds the bumper into nothing. Sam's head hits the passenger window and it spiderwebs. Luckily, the logging truck has passed us because we are forced into the intersection. I do not want to get out and check the damage. My neck is killing me, but I grab the stick and force it into first and hit the gas.

I pull away from the Dodge. Steam rises out of the grill of the big truck. My back bumper drags on the ground and after a few feet it tears off and falls to the asphalt. Several seconds later the airbags blow. What the hell? That was a little late! It scares the shit out of me and I let out a scream. It sounded like a gun went off and the hard rough fabric scratches the hell out of my forearms. The passenger airbag hits Sam in the face. It knocks his glasses off and gives him a bloody nose. I have swerved into oncoming traffic so I jerk the wheel back into my lane. We start to slide. I tap the brakes and try to correct our course. An oncoming car clips into my rear quarter panel. It helps straighten us out at least.

I make a hard right. I am trying to get back onto Sandy Boulevard, because it is a straight shot all the way to the Oregon/Washington border. Sam picks his glasses up off the floor and sees that they are broken, snapped right in half.

"Oh no," he grumbles. I know it is a big deal. He is almost blind. Sam needs these glasses. I remember I have duct tape in my glove box. I reach over his lap and pop the door open. I grab the tape and toss it to him.

"Here, can you fix them?"

"I'll need another set of hands," he says.

"Pass them back here, we'll do it," Tracy speaks up from the back. Sam passes the glasses back with the tape. I am coming up to the Sandy intersection. There are shops on both sides of the street and people are looting. Why would they risk going out to steal a pack of socks, toilet paper or a six-pack of beer if it meant you could die? Humans act so weird when the shit hits the fan.

"Where are we going, Dude?" asks Devon.

"Home."

"My pad is in West Lynn," he says slowly.

"My kids are in Lake Oswego," Tracy pleads.

"I can stop here and let you out if that's what you want," I do not mean to sound like a dick, but my emotions are running hot. "You hopped in my car. I can't drive to West Lynn right now!"

The intersection looks clear so I gun it and hang a left onto Sandy heading east. The second I enter the crosswalk someone runs out in front of me. He slams hard onto my hood,

—

rolls up and destroys my windshield. His bones snap, skull cracks, and joints fold backwards. He flies off the roof and lands face down in the street. This guy is all jacked up. I hit the brakes and come to a stop. We look out my back window at the body on the ground. He is really hurt but not infected.

"FUCK!" I punch my deflated airbag. Seconds later a pack of infected are on him.

"GO! GO!" Devon and Tracy yell from the backseat. Again I slam into first gear and gun it.

My windshield is completely busted. I can't see out of it. I roll down the window to stick my head out. Normally this would seem insanely dangerous, now it feels like suicide. We are getting close to the hospital. I know this because I have lived here my whole life. Besides being a native of Portland, I could tell we were close because of the amount of infected on the street. I swerve to miss them more than the parked cars that litter the road. I drive quickly, close to fifty in a thirty-five zone with my head out the window. My brain works overtime trying to process everything it sees.

I am a lucky man, living in the beautiful Pacific Northwest; I have not gone to war, lived through a natural disaster or seen death up close before. The most exciting thing I have every done, where my life was slightly in danger, was a visit to Six Flags in California. I rode a coaster called the Goliath and I screamed until my voice went hoarse. I am sheltered, pampered and soft. I am not used to seeing skinless humans eating other near skinless humans.

As I speed down the road I witness unbelievable violence and destruction. A blue sedan drives head on into a gas station and it explodes into a fireball. A nasty pack of infected humans tear the arm off an old woman. A pickup pops up onto the sidewalk and takes out a family trying to get into a clothing store. A torso crawls out into the street; its intestines and spine dangle from its severed waist. A man stands in the street with a rifle, opening fire on anything that moves. He must not hear anything because he is obliterated by a Portland City dump truck. A live human runs across the street while he is on fire. An infected digs into a baby stroller. The worst, the worst is the people falling. People are falling from the high-rise buildings on my left and right. It is raining bodies. I can't tell if they are infected before they hit the ground. They could be committing suicide. Jumping to avoid changing into one of them. Jumping because they think they might make it. Jumping because they think this world is over. Who knows, all I know is a person should not have to see this kind of gore. One of the jumpers lands on the road right in front of us and my car goes over what is left of the body. It sounds and feels like I hit a speed bump at fifty miles an hour.

"What the hell was that?!" Sam can't see five feet in front of us.

"It was a person! They're jumping from the buildings!"

"Why?"

"I don't know!" I yell at him.

I finally get past the high-rises. There are no more bodies falling to the ground.

"Here," Devon hands Sam's glasses to him. They have a good amount of duct tape on them. Now Sam really looks like a nerd. I turn away from the road and look at Sam. The glasses should work and he even gives me a smile. I can't imagine all of this and not being able to see on top of that. I would go nuts. My head is still out the window so I can see. I know I should not have looked at Sam. I don't know why I needed to see how bad he would look now with half a roll of duct tape on his glasses, but I did. At the same time Sam's giving me a smile for his fixed specs, a large van hits us on the passenger side. Everything goes black.

I wake up to Devon screaming. My neck hurts like hell. I might be seriously injured. My head was still out the window when we got hit. Even louder than Devon, the van's horn is blasting. The driver must be laying on it dead. I get my eyes open. My side of the car is smashed up against a brick wall. I think it is the post office, I can't see from here. The passenger's side is caved in. I look back to see what the hell Devon is carrying on about and my neck can barely turn to look. Devon has his back up against his window. His leg is up in the air with his boot against Tracy's face. She has a large chunk of metal through her chest and is covered in blood. She must have bled out while I was knocked unconscious. She has turned and is trying her best to get a bite out of Devon. Sam's glasses have been knocked off again and his eyes are closed. Blood pours out the back of his head.
"Sam!" I yell.
"Get me out of here!" Devon panics.
Tracy pushes on his leg and his foot almost slips off her face but he readjusts and gives her cheek another good kick back against the grill of the van. I look back at Sam and his eyes are open. He bares his teeth. His

eyes are black. He is gone. Before I say anything his arms reach out for me. His safety belt is the only thing that saves me; it is caught around his neck. When he lurches forward it stops his progress and gives me the second I need. I grab Sam by the throat. He is stronger now than before. I have a hard time keeping a grip on him.

"Sam, stop it!" he is not listening. He has changed. This is not my friend anymore. I grip his throat. The horn on the van stops blaring. The driver is awake or he is turned. I squeeze his throat and readjust my hands. My fingers slip into the base of his skull. I can feel his brain.

"Sam, please!" I know he is not there but I love this man. He was my best friend for the last ten years. He was the best man at my wedding. He got me the job and taught me sales. I squeeze, twist and push his head up and back. The bones snap in my hands. His body goes limp. He is gone.

"I killed him." I whisper. I can't breathe. Why? No! No! My brain screams while I can only whisper.

"Dude!" Devon's voice pulls me out of my downward spiral. I have got to keep moving.

I pop the trunk of my car and grab my keys out of the ignition. I remembered that I have my tool belt in there from when I helped my mother-in-law put up a fence in her backyard. It is a very tight fit between the roof of the car and the brick wall. I fight to get out of my window and up onto the roof of my car. The driver of the van has turned. It looks right at me while punching the windshield. I climb down the back of my car. The trunk is smashed in and jammed shut. I pull up on it but it is stuck. The driver has punched its way through the windshield, the glass ravages its hand, and flesh strips away and hangs off the bones. It crawls through the glass. I step back and give the trunk a hard kick right on the lock and it pops open. I dig and find my tool belt, grab the hammer and pull it out of the metal loop.

My dad gave me this hammer when I got my first house. I am not super handy and do not build that much. The hammer looks new even though it is ten years old. I climb back on the trunk of my car and hit the back window with the hammer. I keep hitting the window until it smashes out.

"Devon, push her over here!" He forces her head towards me. Tracy was so pretty. Now she is a wreck. I swing down into the car, and my hammer gets her right in the forehead. I have to work the nose of the hammer back and forth to get it out of her skull. Behind me the van driver has pushed his head and shoulders through the window. The sharp glass has scalped him and exposed his collarbones. I get the hammer out of Tracy's skull and turn fast and deliver a killshot to this motherfucker that killed my friends and wrecked my car. Its head caves in. I am sprayed with blood. Devon climbs out the back window and joins me on the roof.

"That's disgusting," he rubs the tears from his eyes. "Now what?" All of my clothes are sopping wet and now my face is coated in blood. We climb down off the roof of my car. I have to kick the back of the trunk again to get it to open. There is not much in there. An old busted football, some dirty socks, a tire pump, one old dress shoe and a boom-box radio from the late eighties. It is all junk. Crap I should have thrown out years ago. Why the hell am I holding onto this stuff? The weirdest thing in there is a crinkled up Playboy from the nineties. I don't remember who was on the cover because it was torn off years ago. I am not sure why I kept it. I have owned a smartphone for a couple years now and that is my main source of female nudity. I grab my tool belt and pull out the two largest screwdrivers. I tuck them both into my pants.

"Dude, what the hell is going on? I think it's a terrorist attack," he nods his head at me.

"I don't know what it is. We need to get off the street," I wipe some of the blood off my face. My eyebrows are soaked. There is so much blood; I wonder if it could make me sick. I snatch up the old dirty sock and rub it all over my face to get the blood off.

"I read online, a couple weeks ago, about this monkey that came back from the dead. You think it's that?" A car crashes into a telephone pole on the other side of the street.

I duck down from the scare, "I don't know. I doubt this is all from a monkey," I scan the area from this crouched position. Cars crash into each other, bodies litter the street, a horde of infected is growing only blocks away. Dead monkeys or terrorists. These are my only two options for why the world went crazy today?

In the building behind us a gun goes off. This building is a post office, I was right. The big front window of the building explodes after another gunshot. It sounds like there are a bunch of infected in there. I step closer to the window. I want to see if anyone needs help. The second I get close to the

window an infected postal worker reaches out
and grabs for me.

Chapter 5

It is my first up close look at a human that is missing its nose and an eyeball. Half of the digits are missing from its hands. His face looks like a muscle chart from seventh grade biology class. Its good eye has gone black with blood. He still has a full mailbag over its shoulder, throwing it off balance. It stumbles forward as it tries to grab me. I knock away its reaching arms with a forearm block. The hit knocks it even more off balance and it falls down onto the windowsill. I give it another good shove and the shards of glass sticking out of the busted window tear up its torso. The glass rips through its skin and opens up its guts. Its intestines spill out onto the tile floor. The smell hits me right away. I feel like I just got slapped in the face with a slaughterhouse. I grab my nose and pinch my nostrils closed. There is another gunshot from inside the building and the bullet rips in and out of this monster's skull. The shot came from a normal looking housewife. I don't know what kind of gun it was but it looks like a cannon in her little hands. She gives me a nod and then turns back into the building.

"Hey, where are you going?" I yell after her, but she is gone.

Devon grabs my arm and gives it a tug. He points across the street. There is a hand beckoning us. It is inside a sporting goods store. Whoever it is has the security cage door open wide enough for their arm to fit through. The arm waves us over.

"Come on," Devon urges me. I lead the way across the street. I am in a full sprint. I can feel Devon right on my heels. When we get to the door the gate slides open and we fly through the opening.

The gate slams shut behind us. My eyes take a second to adjust. It was a sunny spring day outside and the lights are out in this store. I turn to see whom I need to thank for the rescue and he is a heavyset man in his late fifties. He sports a bad comb over and has blood on his clothes.

"Thank you. We appreciate it."

"Yeah. I saw what happened."

"Is there a back way out of here bro?" Devon looks around.

"Yeah, but you don't want to go that way," the guy pulls out a baseball bat and cracks Devon on the back of his head. He falls to the ground and is out cold.

"What are you doing?" I demand as I rush to Devon's side. The man pulls out a gun. It is a snub nose revolver. The kind you would see a cop carry in a seventies TV show. I see where he got the blood from, on the ground behind the counter there are four people laid out dead.

"What the hell?" I am stunned.

"Put your hammer down and give me your wallet!" he commands. The dead are obviously store employees.

"You're robbing us?" I put my old hammer down on the countertop.

"Give me your wallets!" he moves closer.

"You killed these people?! You have any goddamn idea what's going on out there?!"

"I don't give a fuck what's going on out there. I want your money!" he takes a step closer. My heart rate rises with every move he makes. I pull out my wallet and hold it up.

"You're gonna kill me for three dollars and a credit card with a five hundred dollar spending limit?"

He takes another step. He is very close now. I toss the wallet right at his face. It hits him in the nose and he flinches. At the same time I reach out and grab his wrist. I twist, so that I am pushing the gun away from my body. I stomp on the top of his foot. I feel the bones break under my heel. He screams and pulls the trigger. The gunshot is deafening. The round sails across the showroom floor and a football on a shelf explodes. I have a good grip on his wrist so I hit him in the face with my elbow. His nose turns to pulp and blood cascades down his face. He tries to pull his hand back and away from me, I go with it and angle the gun right for his chest. The gun goes off again. The shot hits him right in the heart. We lock eyes. Smoke crawls up his chest from the bullet wound and the tip of the gun. I smell his burning flesh. The life drains from him. I step off his foot and let go. I take the gun away from him as he falls to the floor with a flat thud.

I get a lot of compliments in my Krav Maga class about my speed. Fast punches and fast ducking skills. Not a world-class athlete, but against the "Average Joe" I am fast. It was nothing I worked at, I always had fast hands, but I have never moved this fast before. I have never done anything like this. It is not something you learn in a three-hour-a-week class.

He is dead and I killed him. I had to. Right? I don't feel bad about it. I felt worse when I ran over that guy ten minutes ago. What is happening to me? I cried once because I killed a bird that had landed on our back

porch. It had a broken wing so I put it out of
its misery. This asshole had it coming. I
click open the cylinder on the gun. Each
casing has a small puncture in it. That was
his last shot. I drop the gun to the floor. I
pick my wallet up, go to Devon's side and try
to wake him. I shake him by the shoulders and
he wakes up. He looks at the dead man on the
ground next to me.

"What happened, Dude?"

"He tried to mug us."

"And you killed him?"

"Yeah."

I sit him up, now he can see the dead
people behind the counter. I get Devon to
stand and we look around the place. It is a
BIG 5 sporting goods store. By the front desk
there is a small refrigerator full of water
and sport drinks. I never had lunch. I
definitely have not had enough water. If I
can't find a car I am going to have to walk. I
go to the fridge, pull out a water bottle and
pour it over my head to clean off the blood. I
grab another bottle and drink down all twelve
ounces in one long gulp.

"You're looting?" Devon accuses. I still
have my wallet in my hand. I pull out a dollar
and lay it on the counter. Devon takes a hard
swallow. He is thirsty too. I lay down a
second dollar, open the fridge again and toss
him one. Seconds later we hear the sound of
bodies moving. It is coming from behind the
counter. The dead staff members have turned. I
look over the counter and they are almost to
their feet.

"Shit!" I back away from the counter and
pick up my hammer. One of them is up and turns
for me. She was a young Hispanic girl, around
eighteen, with black hair and braces. She was

shot in the stomach by that asshole. She takes a step toward me and I swing the hammer. I catch her in the temple. The nose of the hammer sticks again and as she falls the handle slips from my grip. The other three are now standing. One is a mid forties manager type and the other two look like high school jocks. I reach for the screwdriver tucked in my belt. I pass one to Devon. The manager has his arms straight out and he tries to grab my shoulders. His teeth snap, his head twitches back and forth.

I am used to fighting someone who has their hands up and in tight to protect their face and body. They move light on their toes. I usually have to watch out for either punches or kicks coming at my head and body. Fighting this guy is very different. His only weapon is that mouth. I quickly step up and between his outstretched arms and drive that screwdriver up through his chin and into his skull. I see the switch get flipped in his brain. His body drops right to the floor. This time I keep a better grip on the screwdriver and pull it from his jaw.

One of the jocks has Devon on the ground and the second one already has his hands on me. I give it a hard shove to the chest and it stumbles backwards, slamming against the counter. Before it can regain its balance, I jam the screwdriver into its jaw and skull.

"Get it off me!" Devon fights from his back. I pull the screwdriver out of its jaw and step quickly over to Devon on the ground. He flails wildly. He stabs the screwdriver into its shoulder, chest, arm and neck. None of his stabs do any real damage and the infected doesn't seem to notice. I step right behind the infected and grab it by its hair. I pull its head back hard as I slide the screwdriver into the base of its skull. Again its like I flipped a switch. Its body goes limp instantly. I use the handle of the screwdriver and its hair to pull it off of Devon.

"Thanks, dude," he gasps. I put out my hand to help him up. He grabs it and I lift him to his feet. As he gets up I look him in the eyes. I see the change on his face. The fear takes shape before he can get the words out. I feel hands on my neck.

It is my heavyset friend with the gun. He is back and he is hungry. I feel his grip tighten on my neck and his body and mouth are not far behind. My reflexes take over. In one move, I tuck my head forward and slap at his hands. This loosens its grip on my neck and I fire an elbow straight up and back. The hard part of my elbow smashes into its jaw and it slams shut. Its teeth break in its mouth. I twist out of its grip and face the monster. It opens its mouth, half its tongue and a bunch of teeth fall out, roll down his belly and fall to the floor. Its jagged, bloody mouth snaps open and shut. It is something straight out of a nightmare. I step close again and drive that screwdriver deep into its chin. He joins the others on the floor. I don't get it. They were dead. You can beat them, stab them, shoot them, set them on fire, peel the skin from their face and nothing. They keep coming at you, but one little stab to the brain and off go the lights.

"Wow, dude you really killed the hell out of those things," he rubs the back of his head.

"Please stop calling me dude or bro. I hate it. You sound like a stupid kid when you

talk that way," I take a deep breath and turn
away from him. I am exhausted. My nerves are
shot. I feel like shit for calling him stupid.
I need a cup of coffee, a shot of whiskey and
a large cold beer. I grab a few more waters
from the fridge, a couple packs of jerky and
Snickers bar. I am starving. Well, North
American man starving. That means I have not
eaten anything for the last five hours. I see
a display of folding camp chairs. I plop
myself down in one and tear open the Snickers.
I open the water and take a swig. "I'm sorry.
You're not stupid. I just re-killed five
people and I'm really hungry,"

"It's alright. My dad says that all the
time to me. I mean he calls me stupid. He's a
dick. I don't want to talk about it," his head
drops. I really feel like an ass now.

"Hey, grab a seat, and get some food,"
Devon pulls out a Mountain Dew and grabs
himself a few Snickers. He plops down on a
chair beside me. I finish off my chocolaty
snack and open the jerky. I look down at my
legs and feet. I am wearing dress shoes with
very slick soles. My pants are polyester dress
slacks. They are cheap and I never have to
iron them, but it is like wearing a plastic
bag on my legs. This is the wrong attire for a
ten-mile hike. I will sweat too much in these
pants. I might slip and fall in these shoes.
Or worse, twist my ankle. I finish off the
first bottle of water. This store is a jackpot
of supplies. When I first ran in I did not
realize what kind of store this was. Now I
feel blessed by the gods. I quickly eat a few
more bites of jerky, finish off the second
bottle of water, get up and walk the aisles.

"Are you shopping du...?" Devon stops
himself from finishing his sentence.

"I can't make it home dressed like this and armed with hammers and screwdrivers."

"So we are looting then?"

"Well there's no one to ring us up," I cruise the aisles and spot the back wall of the store. It has a selection of boots.

He has a mouth full of Snickers as he talks, "Cool, I've always wanted to loot. Like, just a little looting not enough to go to prison."

"What size shoe do you wear?"

"Nine."

"I'll get us some boots," I grab a pack of hiking socks and head for the back room where they keep their footwear.

I flip the light switch on the wall. The back room of the Big 5 lights up and I find a stack of boxes labeled North Face. I pop open a box of size elevens and pull out a set of waterproof hiking boots. These things retail for like two hundred bucks. When I put them on they will be the most expensive shoes I have ever worn. These boots remind me of Sam and his closet full of expensive shoes, like a lady would buy and collect. Sometimes I would joke and call him "Sex Sam and the City." Because he had a collection like the character Sara Jessica Parker played. I think he said one time, he had somewhere around thirty thousand dollars worth. I couldn't believe it. How was that possible? He said he had been collecting them since he was in college. He had like a hundred pair of shoes and most of them were over three hundred bones when he bought them. No matter how many times he explained his collection to me it always sounded over the top. I own about five pairs of shoes, one for work, one to workout, sandals, work boots and one pair of Converse

Chuck Taylor's that I wear around the house. It was such a funny, silly, Sam thing to collect, but he loved them. I pull the boots from the box and I realize that I am crying. The reality has sunk in. I killed my best friend, but only after he had already died once. I think I am going to throw up but I just ate and drank all that water, I don't want it to go to waste, so I fight it. I force a hard swallow. I push all the thoughts about what has happened and what I have done down deep into my soul. I will think about it later. I will cry later. I will throw up later. Now, I have to get ready and go save my girls. I wipe the tears from my eyes and I clear my nose. I don't want Devon to know I was crying. Not that I am ashamed, I was crying in the car not even ten minutes ago, but I can tell he is rattled and on the edge. He needs me to be strong so he feels safe. That will help him be strong. Panic breeds panic. I get myself together and I step from the back room with our new boots.

"We need new pants, shirts and a backpack."

"Are you serious?"

"Yes."

"Sweet," I toss him his boots. I find a pair of camo cargo pants that fit. I pull off my work shoes and dress socks. Devon goes to work on his third Snickers and has not moved from the chair.

"Move your ass. We need to hit the road before more of those...people find us in here." I drop my slacks down to my ankles. I am standing in the middle of the store in my underwear with five dead bodies on the ground and this kid keeps filling his face with candy.

56

"Move it!" I use my "dad voice" and then he snaps too. He hops out of the chair. Before I put my new pants on I notice on the shelf a pair of spandex shorts that hold a cup. I have the same brand for my Krav Maga class. I didn't wear a cup for the first month of class. I thought it would be uncomfortable to do the cardio part in class with a big plastic thing between my legs. After I took a real hard shot to the balls and I couldn't move for five minutes, I went out and bought the cup. I remember when I was buying it the lady at the counter said there was no return policy for this kind of equipment. I would hope there is no return policy for jock straps. I would hate the idea of wearing another man's used nut shield. The memory makes me smirk.

I grab the box and make sure it is the right size. I put spandex shorts on and slip the plastic cup into position. I have no idea what I might face out there, but I do know that if you get hit right in the dick or balls you can't move for a very long time. I would hate to die because I could not move after I got hit in the grapes.

I slip on the new pants and the cotton feels so much better against my skin than the polyester dress pants. I get the thick socks on and slide my feet into the new boots. They feel great. There is a black long sleeve Under Armour shirt on the rack and I grab it. It is the kind meant for football so it has little pads on the shoulders and elbows. I pull off my tie and button up shirt. I pull the new shirt over my head and it fits great. I find a light camo-hunting jacket and grab that too. I grab two sets of shin guards from the soccer section and strap them on my shins and forearms. This should help against those biting bastards.

In the last corner of the store is a display of guns and knives. I step up to the counter and look over the twenty or thirty rifles and shotguns. I have not shot a rifle or shotgun since I was in the Boy Scouts, that was twenty-three years ago. The last gun I shot was a year ago and it was a handgun my brother helped me buy. The two of us shot off a couple hundred rounds the first day I got it and I was a terrible shot. Even my brother said there was only so much practice could do to help with my aim. My body was blessed with quick hands, but cursed with horrible aim. My wife Karen was a better shot with the handgun. Still I need more protection if I am going to make it home. I go behind the counter and try to take down one of the shotguns, but it is locked into the display. I look over at the dead manager on the ground.

"Devon, check that one for keys," I point.

I had not been paying attention to Devon but obviously he was behind me the whole shopping adventure, he is slipping on the same jacket as me in addition to everything else I chose to wear. He also straps on the same set of soccer guards to his limbs. We look like twins. Great. I don't know why it matters but the idea of us rolling down the street dressed exactly the same embarrasses me. Even if the world is going to shit I do not want to get teased by the infected for looking like a couple of dorks. Devon stops walking my way and makes a sad face. It is clear that he doesn't want to touch the dead guy's body. I stare at him, waiting for him to comply with my request. It is a mini staring contest. One

I am not about to lose. Devon's a good-looking young man. He is a couple inches shorter than me and about forty pounds lighter with a clean-shaven face and big bright eyes. Someone might mistake him for my much younger brother. He doesn't say anything. He only shakes his head no. He really doesn't want to touch that dead body.

"Come on. He's dead. Get the keys." I try asking more like a friend than a boss. He slowly walks over to the body and digs through the man's pants pockets and pulls out the set of keys. He tosses them to me and I find one that looks like the lock. It pops open and I pull down the shotgun.

"Shotguns. Sweet. Do you know how to shoot it?" he asks.

"No. Not really. There must be instructions around here." The gun feels heavy in my hands. The side of the stock reads Remington 870. It is all black and has a pistol grip. I try and slide the thing that cocks it. I don't even know what that part is called, but it doesn't move. I pull open a couple of the drawers that sit below the display and finally find one that is full of little books. I sift through the books, find one for the Remington 870 and start reading. Look at me. I am such a nerd. I don't know how to use this stupid thing and I am reading the instructions. Movies make it look so easy. They pick up a gun and know everything about it. The first thing it mentions is eye safety that reminds me to grab some safety sunglasses. I hate going outside without sunglasses. On the first page of the book it lists the Ten Commandments of Firearm Safety.

Number one. Always keep the muzzle pointed in a safe direction. I notice as I read it that I have the muzzle pointed right at Devon. I move the gun away from him.

Number two: Firearms should be unloaded when not actually in use. I look at the gun. How do I tell if it's loaded?

Number three: Do not rely on your gun's safety. I do not see where the safety is. Oh, here on the side by the trigger. I can't tell if it is on or off.

Number four: Be sure of your target and what is beyond it. I didn't even think about that. What if I shoot this gun at one of the infected and hit someone else?

Number five: Use proper ammunition. I think this is a twelve gauge. I look on the shelf and grab a box of rounds.

Number six: If your gun fails to fire when the trigger is pulled, handle with care. I didn't know that could happen. I could be facing down a pack of infected people and the gun doesn't fire. Then what? I throw the gun at them?

Number seven: Always wear eye and ear protection when shooting. Check, I already have a nice pair of sunglasses I just helped myself to. I look over at Devon and he has the same pair on. Damn it.

Number eight: Be sure the barrel is clear of obstructions before shooting. Does it want me to look down the barrel? Rule one was to point muzzle in a safe direction, that doesn't sound safe.

Number nine: Do not alter or modify your gun and have it serviced regularly. Well I don't have to worry about that since I don't know how to modify or service.

Number ten: Learn the mechanics and handling characteristics of your firearm.

The more I think about it this gun might
not be a good idea. It is loud, that will draw
attention. Someone might shoot me for carrying
a gun down the street. It only holds six shots
and if I run into a large group of them I will
not be able to reload it fast enough. I read a
little further and see that red sticking out
on the safety means it is ready to fire and
that there is a locking button I have to press
to get the pump thing to move. I press the
button and pull on the pump and it slides
back. Now I see where the rounds go so I try
to load one. It is really hard to get them in
there. You have to really push it into the
bottom of the gun. I load the six shots that
it holds and pull the pump part back and
forth. It loads a round into the chamber. It
feels really cool when I do it. I feel how
heavy the gun is and how heavy the box of
twelve rounds feel in my hand. I could maybe
carry sixty rounds and feel completely weighed
down by it. Plus, I need to fill the backpack
with some food and water.

"I don't think this shotgun is a good
idea. We need another plan,"

"No shotguns. That's weak."

"They're just too heavy and hard to
reload."

"Yeah. I guess. It's still weak."

I look around for a better idea and see
the display case with the knives in it. I see
it. A few racks over is a wooden walking
stick. It is about five and a half feet tall
and has a nice polished finish. I pull one off
the rack. It feels good in my hands. It is a
solid piece of wood. It has a lanyard so I
slip my hand through the string and hold the
walking stick with both hands.

"You're going to take a stick over a shotgun? Double weak," Devon shakes his head.

"No. I'm going old school," I grab a roll of black athletic tape from a rack on my way back to the knife display. I use the manager's key to open the case and pull out the most expensive knife in there. This thing is ten inches and the blade feels razor sharp. I lay the walking stick on the counter and start to wrap the athletic tape around the tip of the walking stick and the handle of the knife.

"Grab one for yourself," I get the knife wrapped up tight and it feels solid. I push the blade down into the carpet and it does not move or wiggle at all. I wrap some of the tape around the base and the center of the walking stick to give it a little better grip so my hands will not slip. I make one for Devon too.

I grab a backpack, one of those with the water bladder built into it. I open four bottles of water and fill the bladder. They also have some of those Five Hour Energy drinks and the little electrolyte packets that you pour into water. I add two of the packets to my water. I down a Five Hour Energy now and put three in my jacket pocket. There's a display case of Zippo lighters, I grab one with an American flag on it and drop it into my pocket. I also put a few more bags of jerky and Snickers into the pack. I find a little medical kit and toss that in there. Everything I grab and load into the pack, Devon does the same. He makes sure that whatever I have he has. The last thing I throw in there is the hammer that my Dad got me. It was not the best in a fight but I might need it later. Now the pack weighs about thirty pounds. I strap a few more fixed blade knives to my belt and a machete. I can really feel the weight of everything on my body. I wish I were in better shape.

"Okay, I'm almost ready to go. We need to test these spears first," I tell Devon.

"Test them on what?" he muscles his backpack up onto his shoulders. I point the spear at the dead bodies on the ground.

"That's so wrong. That's so, so wrong. We can't do that. It's not right," Devon pleads.

"We have to make sure that the tape will hold. We'll do it to the asshole that tried to murder us," I motion for him to go first. He shakes his head, no. I really don't want to do this either but I don't want the knife to fall off the first time we face one of those infected people. I take a deep breath.

"Fine, I'll go first," I walk over to the body and step over its legs. I raise my spear into the air and jam it down into the body. A large spurt of blood shoots from its body and covers Devon's new boots. I pull the blade out and another spurt of blood follows. It works great, better than I thought it would. I try slicing at something. I swing the spear down at a nearby volleyball and the knife splits it in two.

"That was really cool, dude! Sorry. I didn't mean to call you dude. Sorry I did it again."

"It's fine, just keep them to a minimum."

He nods his head at me, "I will. I promise. I'm gonna try the spear," he steps up to a mannequin. He staggers his feet, like you would if you were taking a fighting stance. The mannequin is dressed in a pair of wild colored swim trunks. He stabs at its abdomen. The knife cuts through the plastic body like butter. He almost knocks the thing over. The kid gives me a smile and a nod.

"Sweet," he pulls out the blade and slices at the plastic dude's neck and the head comes clean off, "Wow. These knives are sharp," he stares at the blade. I test it a few more times on my own mannequin. It is dressed in a fishing outfit. I lop both arms and the head off in three quick strikes. Devon chops a folding chair in half. He lets out a little laugh after the thing falls apart. It looks like he is coming around about these homemade spears.

"This thing works like really good. I don't know if they're better than a shotgun, but they're very cool," the kid runs his thumb over the edge of the blade.

"They feel light and deadly. I guess we'll see," I pull and wiggle the blade a little more. It still feels solid.

"Sweet idea," Devon holds out his fist for me to bump it. I shake my head and I raise my hand in the air for him to high five it.

"Old school," he raises his hand to match mine. I give his palm a solid smack. The power comes from the elbow. I really got him. His hand stings, I can tell, but he acts tough in front of me. When he turns away to secretly rub the soreness from his palm. I take the opportunity to do it too.

I feel good. I am scared as hell to open that door and step out into the city. I realize I have one last thing to do before I go.

"Bathroom break," I tell Devon.

"Yeah, I gotta take a whiz," he puts down his spear. I lean my spear up against the counter next to his.

"Dibs on the guys bathroom," I move quickly to get there first.

"You can't call dibs," he tries to catch up but it is too late. I jog to the restroom and catch a glimpse of myself in a mirror. I look like a weekend warrior or a silly yuppie with a new hobby. I get to the door first.

"Use the little girls room," I tease him. The kid rolls his eyes and enters the ladies bathroom. I can feel the Five Hour Energy start to course through my veins. It makes me want to run and I get very talkative. I had become addicted to these over the years and would take one before every class to get pumped so I would push myself harder and get a better workout. I finish first and head back into the showroom floor. I grab my spear and stand by the window and wait for Devon. I don't see any cars traveling down the street. Maybe the police have things under control. Devon has finished and exits the bathroom. He picks up his spear and meets me by the front door.

"Are you coming with me? Or taking off on your own? I'll support whatever you choose," I hope he comes with me. I can't imagine fighting these things all by myself. He needs to choose. I can't be the one that forced him to come and then have him hate me for it. He thinks for a minute or two. I don't want to rush him.

"I'll miss my Mom," a tear forms in his eye and he swallows hard. "but, I won't miss my Dad," he brushes away the tear. I slide on a pair of wide receiver football gloves and my new safety sunglasses. I hand him the matching pair of gloves. Why not keep this thing going and look like total twins. He slides them onto his hands. I hold my hand out at chest level. He grabs it and we bro hug. We slap at each other's backs. His hand shakes with fear. I am scared too. I do not want to step out this front door. I stop hitting his back and pat him on the shoulder before I let go of his hand.

"We'll be okay. I promise," I don't know why I said that. I can't promise shit. I have no idea what is out there, "you ready?"

"Nope," he slides on his matching set of sunglasses. I unlock the gate and slide it back. I push the door open, pop out my head to look around. That is when the smell hits me. The absolutely disgusting smell of the dead.

"Goddamn it," I curse.

Chapter 6

There is a horde of infected outside and they have seen me pop my head out of the door. We can't hang out at this sporting good store all day. We have to make a run for it. Across the street is a German themed restaurant. It takes up a full city block and the outside is designed to look like an old Bavarian building. Between the restaurant and us it is clear. We have to move fast before the horde of fifty is on us. I take off running. Devon is right behind me. I hope I can keep up with him. I can see us getting caught in a pinch, if he has the chance to run, he might leave me behind. I am halfway across the street heading for the front door. One of the infected is on a collision course with me. He looks like he was one of those crossfit guys, always working out, always at the gym, probably a great looking guy before his nose was torn off. I hold out my spear and tighten my grip. I feel like a Spartan. I aim right for its ugly face. The blade hits it and is so sharp that it slides into its skull like scissors through paper. The body goes limp. This time I am ready for it and I pull the spear up into the air. The blade takes its jaw and most of its face off. I don't slow down. I hurdle its body and sprint past the other infected. We run past my smashed up Mitsubishi and I take one last look at my friend Sam. His body sits like he is sleeping in the passengers seat. I wonder what will happen to his corpse? Will I ever have a moment to come back and bury his body properly? Or will he and Tracy sit there and rot for years before someone can clean up this mess.

I get to the restaurant's red double doors and pull them open. Devon skates in behind me and I slam the door shut. The doors are glass from about the waist up.

"That's not gonna hold." I bark.

The horde hits the door. It is a loud impact and we can hear the creak of the wood flexing under the pressure. The windows must be safety glass because they do not break. The infected claw and punch at the windows. These dead people look like starving orphans, pressing their faces up to the bakers display window, wanting nothing more than to eat everything that is on the other side of the windowpane.

"What should we do?" Devon's voice is strained. I look for something to block up the windows. There is nothing. All of the benches are built into the walls.

"Run," I turn and enter the dining area. Tables and chairs are turned over. People's lunches sit half eaten. There doesn't seem to be anyone in the restaurant. We sprint by a table and there is a beautiful untouched sausage on a plate. I grab it, take a bite, and drop the rest on the ground. Damn these guys know how to cook a pig. We hit the bar when we hear the glass break on the front door. There is a large pitcher of beer on the bar. It is still cold, condensation drips down its plastic sides. I need something to wash down that bite of sausage. Plus I might die any second and that beer is going to waste. I pick up the pitcher and take a big drag off of it.

"What are you doing?" Devon races into the kitchen. I slurp down two more gulps and then toss the pitcher over my shoulder. The beer splashes on the ground behind me.

"Oh, that's good." I follow Devon. In the back there is a big door that reads "EXIT." I stop when I see the gas range. "Hold on!"

"What?"

The monsters crash and fall through the front door. They will keep coming after us. No matter how sharp my spear is I can't kill them all. I move to the gas range and turn the knobs on to high. There is no power to the building but the gas still flows. The gas hisses and the rotten egg smell fills my nose. I turn on each of the six big commercial gas burners. I prop the back door open with a garbage can. I pull the Zippo from my pocket and grab a cardboard box from the recycling. I light a corner of the box on fire. The horde stumbles through the restaurant. I stand back from the door.

"Pull that dumpster over here," Devon grabs the big dumpster and pulls with all his might to get it to move. The first of the infected have entered the kitchen. Their bodies mangled, torn and wrecked from whatever horrible death took their first lives. My cardboard box is halfway burned. The kitchen is full of the infected now. Devon has only moved the dumpster a few feet. One of the monsters stands in the doorway. I toss the box over its head and into the restaurant. I dive behind the metal box.

Boom! The back of the restaurant explodes in a fireball. The heat on my body, even being on the other side of the dumpster, feels like I stuck my face in an oven. I peek over the edge of the dumpster. It worked. There is nothing but fire in that kitchen. I breathe a little easier. Maybe we can get ahead of this and the trip home will not be so bad. I wipe the sweat off my forehead and stare into the fire.

"Shit!" I can't believe it.

"What?"

"They're still coming," they look like the Devil's minions with their black skin pulled tight over their mangled bodies. Six of them move in the kitchen. Why am I surprised, it didn't kill the Jiffy Lube guys. They look lost, bumping into each other and into the kitchen counters. At least it will slow them down.

I help Devon up from the ground and we run north from the restaurant. We cross the parking lot. There are a few cars parked back here. I wish I knew how to hotwire one. Another horde has gathered at the intersection. I step out onto the street and pass a sign that reads "DEAD END". Shit, I hope not. The horde has spotted us. I really feel the Five Hour Energy in my body now. I sprint hard away from the horde. An older hippie couple has stepped out of their house and walks out onto their front yard. They look confused when they see Devon and I sprinting towards them dressed like hunters with homemade spears. Their look of confusion changes to horror when they see what is behind us.

"RUN!" The man pushes his wife back towards their front door. Devon and I sprint past their house. I didn't mean for them to go back inside. Their house has a front porch and low hanging windows. It is an old house from the fifties. Those windows will not keep anything out. I look back over my shoulder and some of the infected have split off from our horde and chase after them. The windows

shatter and the man and woman call out for
help.

The sound makes me run faster. I am not
used to running on anything other than a
treadmill. This thirty-pound pack only adds to
the pain. We get to the end of the block and
find ourselves facing a steep hill. The ground
is covered in sticker brush and weeds. We will
never make it up that hill and through the
overgrown brush.

"Look!" Devon points. Tucked in a corner
near an old garage is a flight of stairs. It
is also overgrown with the sticker brush and
tree branches. The stairs lead up and onto the
next street.

I duck under the first tree branch and
get snagged on a thorny bush. It grabs at my
pants and jacket sleeve. I fight through it,
but the little needles poke through and get
into my skin. Even with my soccer protectors
on my arms and legs they still get me. Devon
and I slowly get to the top of the stairs. My
feet feel heavy, like cinderblocks, and my
heart thumps like a heavy metal drummer, fast
and relentless. I pause at the top of the
stairs and look down at the infected. A
thrashed UPS driver leads the pack. His brown
shorts have turned black with blood. A
waitress follows him. She is from the German
restaurant. Her shirt is torn open and one of
her breasts is exposed. Bite marks cover most
of her bouncing C-cup. It is one messy body
after another. They smash through the stickers
and tree branches. Their horribly mangled
bodies are the only things slowing them down.

We have entered into a nice little street
of pretty houses. I step out onto the asphalt.
I am halfway across when I hear tires
screeching on the pavement. A sedan skids

around the corner and it is doing eighty. I lock eyes with the driver. This is it. I am dead. No way is this guy going to stop. He jams on his brakes. I can't believe it. He swerves at the last second to miss us. His sedan smashes into a parked Volkswagen Bug. The parked car pops the curb and slides across the front yard, right for the set of stairs we just ran up. The Volkswagen hits the top of the stairs and it tips over. It is small enough to fit down into the stairwell. The car slides down the concrete and slams right into the horde that is halfway up the stairs. It pulverizes them and crushes their infected bodies. The Volkswagen knocks out the whole horde when it comes to a stop at the bottom of the stairs.

The sedan's front end hits a pile of decorative stones that sit in the corner of the house's yard. The sedan flies into the air and hops over the stairwell. The car comes to a stop at the top of the stairs. It blocks the stairs so that no one can get up or down them anymore. The driver's side door pops open and a man in his forties falls out, landing on his back.

"Damn it!" I can't leave him out here. He wrecked his car so he would not hit us. "Come on," I lead Devon back over to the man on the ground. He has a cut above his right eye and blood drips down his face. When I get close enough and see there is a wound on his forearm. "Did you get bit by one of those things?" He nods his head yes.

"Should we leave him?" Devon pulls at my pack.

"Do you live around here?" I kneel down beside him.

"Down the block," he points in the direction. I reach into his car, pull out the keys from the ignition and put them in my pocket.

"Lets get him up."

"He's gonna turn, right?"

"Help me get him up. We owe him that," I have my arm tucked under his. Devon helps me get the man to his feet. He coughs a fountain of black blood.

"This is a bad idea." We drag the guy, his feet only helping every couple of steps.

"Which house is yours?"

"5166," he burps up more blood. We are a few houses away. About ten houses down from us is an intersection. It is a war zone. There are five police cars parked side by side and the officers are making a stand down there. A S.W.A.T. team pulls into the intersection and joins the other officers. They jump from their truck armed with assault rifles and shotguns. They decimate the ranks of the dead. I lose sight of the action, as we get closer to this guy's house.

He lives in a nice two story with a garage recessed into the ground. We are at the steps that lead up to his front door and he starts coughing hard. It is a violent, blood-spewing, hacking cough. We drag him up the stairs. He is passed out, might even be dead already. We pull his limp body up the flight of stairs and I bang at the front door.

"Open up!" I sound like a cop. I dig in my pocket to find his key. The door opens. A beautiful woman in her forties answers.

"What do you want?" then she sees whom we have in our arms. She cries out in panic. "Brad! What happened?" she opens the front door to let us drag him in.

"He crashed his car down the street. He was still awake when we found him," I tell her as we carry him into the living room and lay him down on the floor. She places a pillow under his head. Their place is well furnished. Beautiful leather couches and expensive artwork on every wall. These two definitely had an eye for design.

"Please call an ambulance!" she begs.

"It won't do any good. He's been bit," she looks at me like I am the crazy one. She doesn't know.

"Lady, there's some kind of infectious disease out there and if you get bit you die," Devon says matter-of-factly then turns to me. "Let's jet."

"Ma'am, I know this sounds nuts, but what he's saying is the truth. It's chaos outside. The emergency services are all down and people can spread this infection through bites. Look at his arm," I point at the bite. She lifts his wrist. The clear bite marks from a human mouth have become green and infected. Pus leaks from the wound. It is swollen, red, and his veins are dark black all over his arm. It will not be long. I kneel down beside her.

"Say your goodbyes, he's about to change," she shakes her head in disbelief with tears in her eyes.

"What do you mean, change?" she asks.

"This is hard to understand but I've seen it happen. He will die. Then he will come back. He won't be the same. He will try to hurt you and anyone around you. We have to leave right now and I have to put the spear...into his skull."

She slaps me hard across the face. Where were my Krav skills there? I let her make full contact with my face. I deserved it. I just told her I want to stab her guy in the skull. My bedside manner is horrible.

"Get out!" she wails. I stand up and rub my cheek. She really got me on the sweet spot.

"Okay," I turn away from her as she sobs over Brad's body. I have to keep moving but if I go this lady is dead.

She cries out in pain. I spin around and Brad has her hand in his mouth. Her bones snap and flesh tear as Brad eats off her ring and pinky finger. I lunge toward them and stab into Brad's head. I get him the first time, but she is missing her two fingers.

"We've got to kill the infection!" I pull her towards the kitchen. I step her up to the sink and kick on the faucet. I hold her hand under the water as she fights against me. Maybe I can keep her from getting infected. The wound on her hand is disgusting. Two white bones twitching in a raw meat sandwich.

"Find some medical supplies and rubbing alcohol!" I yell over my shoulder at Devon. He tears off into the closest bathroom.

"I know it hurts! We've gotta clean it!" Devon comes back with a cheap medical kit and a bottle of alcohol. I turn off the water, reach out for the bottle, snap the lid open and hold it over her hand. "Sorry," I pour out a little of the rubbing alcohol onto her hand. You would have thought I bit another finger off. I cut my hand on a dirty chicken coop I owned three years ago and I put alcohol on that wound. It hurt more than the actual cut. "Get out a wrap and bandage," Devon pops open the medical kit and pulls out the roll of gauze and bandages. "Put some Neosporin on it."

"What?"

"I don't know. It's worth a shot," Devon goes back to her bathroom to rummage through her cabinets.

"I'm going to put a little more on to make sure it's clean."

"Please don't," she can barely talk.

"I have to," I pour out a little more. I make sure I cover every part of the wound. "Fight through the pain," I tell her. Devon comes back into the kitchen with the Neosporin. He squirts a large amount onto the bandage. "I've got to put pressure on your wound so we can stop the bleeding."

"Do it." is all she can say. I hold her up by her arm because she wants to fall to the floor. Devon slides a kitchen chair over from the dining table. I get it under her butt. I take the bandage from Devon and I carefully press it over the wound on her hand. She passes out.

"Hand me the gauze," he hands me the roll and I carefully wrap it around her hand and wrist. I use the whole roll on her to make sure I have enough pressure on it to stop the bleeding.

"Tape," Devon tears off a few bits of tape for me to put on the gauze to hold it into place.

"I think we need more," I reach out my hand and take the tape from him. I wrap it around her wrist like a boxer. "Done," she wakes up. Her face looks like she gave birth to a baby fire truck. "What's your name?"

"Colleen."

"I'm Jim and this is Devon. It's not going to be safe here. Do you have any family close?"

"No. Just Brad," it takes a lot of effort to talk. I pick up the medical box and dig

76

around in it until I find some Tylenol. I pop out the pills.

"No. Vicodin," she says pointing to the bathroom. I motion to Devon to go. He makes for the door.

Seconds later Devon comes back into the kitchen with a little bottle of prescription pills. He hands her one and she downs it with a hard swallow.

"Colleen, we need to get moving. I'm heading North into Vancouver. You can come with us but we need to go now. Do you have another car?"

"No. We don't have a car," her eyes aren't focused and the words come slowly. "We have the Bronco," she slurs. "It's my husband's baby. It's down in the garage."

I pull Brad's keys from my pocket and one of the keys has a custom FB stamped in to it.

"Grab a jacket and let's move."

"Wait," she looks at her bandaged hand. "My ring," I look at Devon and then back into the living room at Brad's dead body.

"Really?"

"Please help me?" she whimpers. I drop my head. This is going to be gross, but I can't leave her and steal her dead husbands Bronco. I pull out one of the knives I have strapped to my hip. I walk over to Brad's dead body and kneel down next to his head. Devon steps into the living room with me. Colleen follows him. I look at Brad's destroyed face. I got him right between the eyes but the blade is so big that it cut into his left eye. I have a thing about eyes. Touching them grosses me out. My Dad wore contacts and I would almost throw up as a kid every time he would put them in. My stomach turns a little so I look away from his eyes and focus on the jaw. I take the back of the knife and slide it between his lips. The metal clanks against the enamel of his teeth. I move the blade back and forth until I get it to slide between his teeth. I pull down to open his jaw. Blood dumps out onto the floor. I jump back a little when the blood pours my way. It reminds me of when I was sixteen and my parents took my brother and me to Disneyland. On our first night there we rode "It's A Small World." It was a horrible ride. Long and boring. If you ever get a chance to ride it, don't. You are trapped on a little boat, floating in gross old water with the same stupid song playing over and over. I am sitting in this little boat with my family and I am wearing my brand new letterman's jacket. I worked really hard to earn this jacket and I was so proud of it. I think it might have only been a month old at this point. The boat rocked and I thought some of the nasty water was going to splash up onto my beautiful jacket. So I jumped. I jumped like a shark was coming to get me. After that my parents loved to tell everyone that I was scared and jumped on the "It's A Small World" ride. I jumped the same way just now. Like the blood was a shark coming to get me.

"I can't do this. You're gonna have to do it. I'll hold it open," I fight back against the puke. She stumbles over to her dead husbands body. With her good hand she digs her fingers down into the blood. I pull on the jaw to open it as far as it will go. She digs down deep almost to her wrist. Tears stream down her cheeks. She gets a hold of something and pulls her hand out of his mouth. It is so coated in blood I can't tell if she has got it. She stands up, walks back into the kitchen and turns on the water at the sink. The water reveals a severed finger with a diamond ring on it. She works the ring off the finger.

"Should I put it on ice? Maybe they can put it back on."

"The hospitals are overrun," I tell her. She nods her head and picks her jacket off the back of a dining chair. She tosses the severed finger into the sink like it was a spoiled hotdog.

"The stairs are down here," she leads the way into a hall. Devon and I follow her down into the tight stairway. At the bottom of the stairs is another door. She opens it and turns on the lights. When I enter the room I am blown away. It is a rebuilt Ford Bronco. I am not a car guy, but it is a good-looking machine. The silver paint looks 3D. The tires are big and knobby. They look like they can climb straight up a wall. This room is a shrine to all things Ford Bronco, old posters, toy cars and books. One of the posters on the wall is of this exact Bronco. It has the year 1974 written across the top of the poster. This guy loved this car and I am about to take it and probably destroy it. We will be lucky if it even makes it to the river.

"What's the plan?" Colleen asks.

"I'm gonna take the side roads and get to Vancouver," I open the door and slide into the driver's seat. She pops open the passenger door. "Get in kid," she says to Devon. He pops the lever on the front seat to get it to fold forward and climbs up into the backseat. I slide the key into the ignition, push in the clutch and turn the key. The V8 roars to life. I click the garage door opener. The door slowly rises. I give the gas a few pumps and the body of the SUV shakes. This thing has got a lot of torque. There is a small pack of infected in the street. A couple of teens and an old woman, all three of them look like they were shot out of a meat grinder.

"What happened to them?" Colleen looks over to me.

"They're infected," I slip it into first and let off the clutch and the Bronco takes off out of the garage. The infected race to meet us.

Chapter 7

I have only driven this car for two seconds and I have already put a dent into it. At this speed the infected bounce off the Bronco's front end. An old lady's arm is ripped off and it lays flat against the windshield. I hit the switch that runs the wipers as I take a right out of the garage. They help push the arm off the window and onto the asphalt. The wipers also do a great job of smearing the blood and gore all over the windshield. I click on the spray and the dark black blood turns pink as the wipers wash the window clean. Colleen covers her eyes. The police have been overrun at the intersection. The cruisers are covered in blood. Infected bodies wearing riot gear mill about in the streets. They make a beeline for us.

"It's worse than…I never would have thought…" Colleen shakes her head.

I take a left to avoid the growing horde. There is an old Catholic church up ahead. Groups of people fight against the infected on the steps. They are armed with bats, hockey sticks and a few machetes. People see the world going to hell and they go to church. It makes sense. The group on the stairs beat the hell out of the infected. They deliver head blow after head blow. The massive staircase that leads up into the church is coated in their black blood.

I check my watch and it is a little after one o'clock. If I can keep this Bronco on the road I will be home in about twenty minutes. On the street a family tries to load their car and a group of infected has spotted them.

"Should we help them?" asks Colleen. I don't answer her. There is no good answer.

Yes, I want to help them, but I can't. I can't stop every time a family is in trouble. I would never get home.

"Holy shit!" I blurt out. A man, completely covered in blood, jogs down the sidewalk with a running chainsaw. He looks like Leatherface in the *Texas Chain Saw Massacre* movie.

"Damn!" exclaims Devon.

"Where's he going?" asks Colleen.

"That's such a bad idea. He's gonna lose a limb," I shake my head.

Every other driveway on the street has a family loading up their vehicle. Where the hell do they think they are going? Does everyone have a safe house that they can bug out to? Like it is safer out here on the street. Here I am trying to get home and they are leaving theirs. If it is like this everywhere then the streets are going to be swamped. The roads are about to become an all you can eat buffet for the infected. The dinner bell is ringing. We are coming up on a large cemetery. I downshift to get ready for a turn, but at the end of the block there is an overturned semi. It lies across the street and blocks my right turn. A big Ford truck is jammed in between the semi and the trailer. The pickup is on fire. The driver of the semi fights to get out of the cab. He gets to his feet and looks around. It is an eight-foot drop to the ground. I look for a place to squeeze by the accident. The truck driver leaps out into the air the second the semi explodes. He is engulfed in flames. He rolls on the ground unable to put himself out. Fire has spread everywhere around the semi truck. All of the brush and trees are going up in flames. I can't turn right anymore. Going left sends me in the wrong direction. A fence surrounds the graveyard that is dead ahead of us. I drop the Bronco into second gear and punch it.

"What are you doing?" Colleen props up in her seat, appalled.

"Shortcut," I answer. We pop the curb at forty miles an hour and smash the fence down. It folds easily under the knobby tires and we zip across the grass.

"You're a crazy man," announces Devon.

"It's gonna save us time," I tell him.

"My Grandpa is buried in this cemetery," Colleen's eyes are drooping.

"I'm sorry," Devon mutters.

"It's okay. He passed when I was a kid. I forget to go see him, even though I live so close," her words come slow and are slurred together. I steal a quick glance over at her. She is a beautiful woman, but what I am looking for are dark veins running up her arm from her wrist. I don't see anything on her. Yet.

I get to the gravel road that runs through the cemetery. There is no infected anywhere in sight.

"Look over there!" Devon reaches into the front seat and points his arm in front of my face. A young girl is under attack. The infected have her on the ground. Wait. Her attackers are not infected they are four teenage boys. Two of the boys fight to get her pants off and the other two pin her arms to the ground. I can't believe this shit. My face goes flush.

"Jim?" Colleen slurs.

I tap the brakes and turn the wheel. I cut back across the graveyard. They are so busy with their disgusting act they don't notice the Bronco. I jam on the brakes and come to a skidding stop.

One of the assholes works to get his little penis out of his jeans. I am so full of rage, I am not thinking straight. I am not thinking at all. I am on autopilot. The ones holding her arms have their backs to me. I quickly step away from the Bronco and I stomp down hard onto one of their lower backs. The hard rubber sole of my boot grinds down his vertebrae. He lets out a high-pitched scream and falls to the ground, clutching his spine. This alerts the other three assholes that I am not here to be friends.

The rest of this happens so fast it is only the click of a few seconds. I hit the one holding down her other arm, with a fast hammer fist. I aim for the top of his sternum. It crunches. He falls to his back gasping. To make sure they don't go anywhere I stomp down on their thighs. You hit someone in the iliotibial band that runs down the side of their femur and they can't walk. I know because I have been kicked there and needed to take five minutes before I could keep going in my class.

The girl on the ground fights back and lands a solid kick. She gives the kid a bloody nose. He falls backwards and tries to crab walk out of here. I take a few quick steps towards him and throw a kick. My boot lands hard in his ass crack. I hit him so hard that he falls on his neck and does a backwards somersault landing on his stomach. He screams like a baby with his face down in the dirt. I drop a heavy knee down onto the back of his neck. It forces his face down deep into the grass. He panics for air. The last one still has his little pee pee hanging out of his

84

pants. I reach out and catch him by the collar of his shirt. Stepping off his buddy as he turns to face me, I have my other knee ready to greet him. My hands are around his skinny neck as my knee hits every square inch of his exposed privates. He doesn't scream. He grunts. I use his neck to slam him to the ground. I come down on this guy and it is all elbows. I keep a tight hold of his throat and hit him in his teeth and nose. Colleen yells my name. It brings me back to my senses. I look at the bloody mess I made. His face looks like raw hamburger meat. I think I broke his eye socket. I get to my feet. The girl works to get her pants on. I have never been in a real fight before. I have only sparred in class. I have forty or fifty pounds on each of these punks lying on the ground writhing in pain, but I am going to count it as a fight that I won.

"You okay?" I already know the answer but I still ask. She kind of shakes her head.

"You got any family?"

She has her pants on and works on her one shoe that fell off. "No."

"Dead?"

"Yes."

"What's your name?"

"Sara," I am still not thinking straight. I have never been this mad before. My wife, family and coworkers tease me about never ever getting mad or losing my cool, but I have never had a day like this. I am a normal husband and father. I sell appliances to people that have first world problems.

"Are you coming?"

"What?" she asks. I walk to the Bronco and pull the lever that releases the front seat so it falls forward.

"Get in."

She moves quickly for the car, pulls her hair back out of her face and readjusts her clothes. She is a beautiful young redhead, about five seven, a hundred and ten pounds and twenty years old. She climbs up and into the back of the Bronco next to Devon. They sit there awkwardly. What is he supposed to say? I climb back into the driver's seat and slam the door shut. I take one last look at the little turds on the ground.

They are kids. What the hell were they thinking? Why aren't they home with their families? Even though I shouldn't feel bad for them I still do. They deserved what they got, but I fucked them up so much they will have a tough time getting back to safety. I might have sentenced them to death. I probably could have scared them away. I didn't have to beat the shit out of them. I didn't have to elbow the kid in the face so many times. I don't know what to think. My moral compass has a magnet sitting next to it.

I punch the gas and head back for the gravel road. Colleen turns around in her seat to face Sara.

"It's going to be okay," she tells her.

"I knew them," Sara gets her seat belt across her lap and clicks the ends together.

"Sweetheart, I'm so sorry," Colleen holds out her good hand and places it on Sara's knee. Devon shifts around in the back seat. He slides a sheathed knife off his belt and hands it to Sara.

"You can have this," she takes it.

"Thank you."

"These knives are awesomely sharp. So like be, careful," Devon nods his head at her.

She reaches over the drivers seat and grabs my shoulder.

"Thank you," she says to me.

"You're welcome," it sounds awkward when I say it. I don't know how to talk to kids. The deeper I get into my thirties the more uncomfortable I feel around them. It is why I struggle to talk with Devon. They make me feel old. I am not old, but they make me feel that way for some reason. "Do you live around here?"

"Yes," she says softly.

"You want me to drop you off?"

"No. It's not safe," she stares out the window.

"You got any place to go?" asks Colleen.

"No."

"You can stay with us," Devon tells her. I look up at the mirror and back at her. I wish I had something I could say to her and help her feel better, but I have nothing.

I head for the farthest northeast corner of the cemetery. There is no outlet back onto the main streets. It is all fenced in. North of the cemetery sits a row of houses and their backyards butt up against the fence.

"I'm gonna go through it," I tell them. "Hold on," I aim for what looks like a space between the houses. I hope I don't hit a parked car or a kid. The fence folds under the weight of the Bronco. A couple of feet later we hit a wood fence. I aim for the spot between the two posts that anchor it to the ground. The two by fours snap and the fence crumbles. We have entered into a small alley that separates the two houses.

At the next intersection there is a burning car in the middle of the street. Gangs of monsters run from house to house looking for their next victims to feed upon. There is a dump truck crashed halfway into a house across the street. A horde of infected has spotted us.

"Keep going, man!" Devon yells.

I punch it and pull away. The street comes to a dead end. There is a row of four-foot high scrubs blocking us from the next street. A parking lot sits on the other side of the bushes.

"Drive over it!" Devon encourages me. I put the pedal down. We blast over the plant divider. An apartment complex sits to our right and a bunch of people are packing up their cars right in front of us. I almost run over a few kids carrying armfuls of toys. What are these parents doing? Strap the kids into the car or leave them in the apartment until it is safe. The horde has entered the lot behind us. I screwed up. Shit. I led the lions to the lambs. Most of the people are single moms and their kids, a couple of old folks. A dozen infected spill out into the lot. I have to fix this. I slam on the brakes and throw the Bronco into reverse and step on the gas. I head right for the infected.

"Get down!"

Devon and Sara duck down under the backseat. A spare tire hangs from the back of the Bronco and it takes the brunt of the impact. The Bronco takes down six of the dead bastards. I mash on the brakes. The tires slide on blood and guts. I grab my spear.

"Come on, kid!" I yell back at Devon. One of the infected lies on the ground under my door, its legs destroyed, but it still grabs and claws up at me. I open the door fast and hard to bang it in the skull. I step out from the vehicle and stab its brains. Devon struggles to cross over Sara's lap but he finally gets out and is right behind me. I lunge at the next infected and slice at its head. The blade takes the cranium off with one easy swipe. Its body falls forward and its neck hole shoots me with, what feels like, every ounce of blood it has to offer. Devon jumps out with his spear and stabs an oncoming infected in the face. His first solo kill.

"Sweet," I tell him. It was all he needed to hear. On the other side of the car the last few infected scratch and claw at the windows. Colleen's first up close look at the infected. She is frozen with fear. I run around the front of the car and I stab the one staring at Colleen. Blood spurts up onto the window. Devon is a second behind me and he takes out the last one. He lets out a battle cry as he cuts the monster's head in two. I scan the parking lot. That was the last one in this area. I turn to face the people.

"Stay off the roads! Find a weapon and get back in your house," I quickly get to the drivers side and let Devon in first. The people stand silent and in shock. They stare at us like we are aliens.

"Move it!" I bark at them. They snap out of it and run back into their houses. I climb back into the Bronco, slam the door shut and get it back into gear. Colleen shakes in her seat. I grab her wrist and pull it towards me. I slide her sleeve back to expose her forearm. There are no black veins.

"What are you doing?" asks Sara.

"She was bitten," I let go of Colleen's arm.

"You let her live?"

"I'm not a doctor. I don't know how this works. I saw a two-minute video on the news.

That's it. She seems fine," I let out the clutch and take off with a lurch. All four tires screech. The lot is empty by the time we get to the street.

"Where are we going?" asks Sara.

"Vancouver. That's where my family is."

"Vancouver? You wanna cross the bridge? With all this shit going on? That's insane," she has snapped out of her haze.

"I have to get to my family. They're in Vancouver. So I'm gonna get across that bridge," I shift into the next gear.

"Maybe you should drop me off," she is restless back there. I pull to the next street. There is a pack of bloodthirsty infected heading for us.

"You want out now?" I ask her. She looks at the angry horde of death.

"No. I'll stay," she says contrite.

There are a few people packing their cars to bug out on this little street. I roll down my window.

"There's a shit ton of them heading this way! You better get moving!" I yell out to the families and then roll my window back up.

"Will that happen to me?" Colleen asks in a low voice. I glance over at her and I shrug my shoulders. Tears pour down her cheeks.

"I don't want to die. I don't want to die! I don'..."

"Knock it off! If you act crazy I'll drop your ass off right here!" my voice breaks and I punch the dash. It doesn't help anyone if I freak out now. I have got to calm down. "I'm sorry. We have to keep it together for a little..." I look over at Colleen. She is zoned in on her forearm. Her veins have gone black.

Chapter 8

Colleen squeezes her infected arm at the elbow.

"NO, NO, NO!"

"Do something!" she pleads.

"She's turning!" Devon panics.

"Pull over!" yells Sara. Colleen coughs up a mouthful of blood. Damn this infection! She spews blood onto her jacket and all over the dash. I slam on the brakes and pull over. She convulses. I get out of the Bronco and I pop the seat forward to let out Devon and Sara. I sprint around to the passenger's side and open the door.

"Colleen?!" I call her. She doesn't respond. I slide my arms under her knees and the back of her neck and I pull her out. I lay her on the grass and take a few steps back. I watch as her eyes go blood red and the skin around her mouth pulls tight. Her whole body shakes violently and blood drains out of her nose and ears. Her eyes turn black.

"We should go," Sara says.

"Should, we finish her?" asks Devon. Nothing about this feels right. I don't know this woman but she seemed like a good person.

"Damn it!" I pull the knife I have on my hip and kneel next to her body. I place my hand on her forehead like you would to test a sick child's temperature. I take the blade and stick it into her jaw and up into her brain. Her body stops shaking and it is over. What am I doing? This is a fucking nightmare. This is a lesson. If you are bitten you have to go. There is no stopping this infection. I should have listened to Devon. No way in hell I will make that mistake again.

"Should we say something?" wonders Devon. I pull the blade from her body and stand back up.

"Go ahead," I mutter. I put the knife back on my hip.

"I don't know, man."

Two guys sprint across the street for the Bronco. Like a dummy I left the keys in the ignition. Both guys are good sized and in their thirties. One of them has bleach blonde hair. I move fast to get back to the driver's side. The blonde one is already halfway into the Bronco when I get to him.

"Get out!" I reach for his belt.

"Fuck you!" he yells over his shoulder at me. I grab his belt and pull him out. As he falls out he throws a punch at me. It almost connects, but I slide my head to the side. It only grazes me. I take a step back so I have a second to think. Devon joins me. I hope he is ready for this. Most fights are over in a minute and all of them end up on the ground. If I end up on my back these two will stomp me to death. The two guys charge. The blonde one throws a few haymakers. I block and duck. The other guy comes at Devon. They punch wildly at each other. Blondie switches from haymakers to uppercuts. He keeps advancing and I take a few steps back. I am pressed against the Bronco and I have nowhere left to go. He lands a hard right on my chin and it rings my bell. I hate being hit. I get hit in class sometimes. It is always on accident, but it hurts so badly. The human face is not designed to take a beating. It is soft and breaks easily. Devon is on the ground getting punched in the head. He is finding out exactly what I am talking about. The poor guy is in big trouble. Damn it. If I can't take Blondie out fast, Devon is going to get killed. Sara moves quickly and stabs the back of Devon's attacker. The guy cries out in pain. She got him right in the shoulder blade. The knife stays stuck in his back. His arms fight to reach back and pull it out.

Blondie throws a straight jab at me. I do a move that I practiced in class over and over again. As his left hand comes straight for my face I push his punch slightly to slide past my face and at the exact same time I throw a straight punch. I aim for his neck. It delivers the most damage to an opponent with the least amount of risk to my hand. It connects. Blondie can't breathe. He grabs his throat. I make sure there is no more fight in him with a hard rising kick to the groin. He falls to his knees. That is the second time I kicked a man's dick today. I guess it is my signature move.

The other guy gets up off Devon. He charges at me, hits me full force and I am slammed up against the Bronco. My head hits the back quarter window. It dazes me. He throws punches at my face. He lands one in my ear and a hook that gets my nose. The cartilage breaks on impact. Pain radiates. Oh baby, does the pain radiate. My sunglasses crack and fall to the ground. Blood drains down into my throat and I start coughing. I try to keep my hands up as he throws punches at me, but I am hurting.

Suddenly he stops attacking me and he screams out in pain again. When he turns around the knife is in a different spot. Sara pulled it out and stabbed him again. This is my chance. I muster everything I have left in me and kick hard into the back of his leg. This sends him to his knees. I quickly reach out and throw my arms around his head. I choke him out by pinching off his carotid artery with my forearm. If you get a good deep choke, you can make someone blackout in a few seconds. I feel his body go limp. My nose kills with every heavy breath I take.

What the hell were these assholes thinking? Trying to steal someone's ride. Then he breaks my nose. I am no Brad Pitt, but I liked my nose and now I am going to look like an old boxer. He fully passes out. I let his body go and it falls forward and lands face down on his blonde friend. I look up at Sara. My eyelids flutter and I can't focus. She pulls the knife out of his body and puts it back into its sheath.

"Thank you," my eyes will not focus and my voice sounds funny with my busted nose full of blood.

"I owed you one," she steps over to help Devon up. I hope that this doesn't become the new form of currency. Violent acts exchanged for more violent acts; you saved me from being raped. Okay. I owe you two stabs in someone's back.

"Help me with him," we grab Devon by the arms and pull him to his feet. He is going to have a black eye and his lip is busted.

"Fuck, that hurt dude. Sorry," he says.

"That's okay," I rinse the blood out of my mouth and then take a big drink of water.

"Lets get the hell out of here," Sara helps him back around to the passenger's side of the car. I get back into the Bronco and lock the door behind me. I look in the rearview mirror and check out my nose. There is a bulge on the bridge. I have seen in movies where tough guys reset the nose easy-peasy. The last thing I want to do is touch it. Devon lies down on the bench. Sara sits up front next to me. She grimaces when she sees my nose.

"It looks broken."

"It's very broken."

"You want me to set it?"

"No," I say instantly.

"Are you going to?"

"No," I say as fast as before.

"It will take two seconds and then we can get going."

"Have you ever done it before?"

"No, I've seen it in the movies."

"You don't know what you're doing," she moves closer to my face with her hands out.

"It can't be that hard. Don't be a pussy."

Who is this girl? She has her hands close to my nose.

"Please don't!" I plead with her.

"Hey! Hold still! You don't want me to fuck this up, do you?" I wince when she touches my nose.

"Please stop! It's fine! I'll be OKAAAAY!" Crunch! This crazy chick reset my nose. Damn it hurts! I look in the mirror and the bulge is gone. My nose is swollen and hurts like hell. Who is this girl? She resets broken noses and will stab a man to save a stranger. "I can't believe you did that!"

"I told you it was easy. Can we go now?"

"Yeah," I look back at Devon. He stares at Sara. It is puppy love. My first impression of this girl is that she chews up and spits out boys like Devon. I hit the gas. I snake my way down some back roads. They seem to be a little quieter. No more stops, I promise myself. I can't take anymore car crashes or punches to the face.

The next intersection we pull up to has an old folks home on the corner.

"Oh no."

"What?" asks Devon.

"It's an old folks home."

"So?"

"Look," he sits up to see. The street if full of old infected bodies. They see us and shuffle our way. If I go through them I will wreck this Bronco. Someone must have passed early this morning and the rest of the poor old people could not do anything to stop them. Oh crap, I remember there is an old folks home not even three blocks from where I live. I am not an ageist, but when people get old and can't take care of themselves it can get gross. Add torn flesh, missing limbs, open night gowns, popped colostomy bags and it gets absolutely disgusting. It would be nice if I could go five minutes without all of my senses being completely bombarded with horrifying, nightmarish gore.

Behind us a diesel engine is moving fast. It is a snow plow. Where the hell did this guy get a snow plow? He tears across the intersection. The big plow is covered in human remains. It absolutely decimates these old bodies. It hits six at a time and doesn't slow down. I look over at Sara and she gives me a half smile. It is so over the top, even though it is incredibly wrong and disturbing, you want to laugh. Only so you don't go completely insane. The plow takes out all of the infected on the street. I hit the gas and follow him. The Bronco slides around on the concrete as I get up to speed. The ground is slick with body fluids. The plow weaves all over the street purposely hitting the infected.

"This guy's like, bat shit insane!" exclaims Devon.

The plow hits a parked car and tears off every metal panel and the door like it was newspaper. We zip down two blocks before I know it. I wish I could follow this guy all the way home. I would be there in ten minutes.

The road comes to an end and the plow slams on its brakes and makes a hard right. It takes down a fire hydrant on the corner. Water explodes into the air and splashes down on us. It covers my windshield with so much water we go blind for a few seconds until I find the controls for the wipers. The next road we pull onto is littered with cars. The people drive like maniacs trying to get home, or leave home, who knows. I thought this guy would slow down now that he is on a main road, but he is going even faster. He weaves in and out of traffic still pulverizing the random infected that try to cross the street.   "He's going to kill someone," I shift into the last gear. I stay with the plow. It is the best lead blocker ever, but I am pushing seventy. The speed limit is only thirty five. My butthole eats the seat every time I pass a car or enter an intersection. There is a major intersection up ahead and it is full of cars. He tears the back and front bumper off them. It makes for a nice opening that we dart through.

The next intersection opens up to a four lane with a median and it has more cars to navigate through. I don't understand why he is driving this way. If he took it slow he would still get where he is going. Why drive like a maniac? The stress of getting into another car crash is not worth following this madman. We have gone thirteen blocks and it only took us a minute to get here. So that is cool, but

Goddamn, slow down you weirdo. He blows apart a few infected bodies. Some of the guts and blood spray up and over the top of the plow and land on our ride. I fire the wipers back up to clear the window.

The plow races through the next intersection and is t-boned by a fast moving fire truck. The unstoppable force has met its match. The fire truck pushes it into another car and the plow tips over on its side. I jam on the brakes. The whole intersection is full of busted vehicles and now I don't have a lead blocker. I search for a clear path that will keep me going in the right direction, but there is none.

Seconds after the plow comes to a full stop on its side the passenger door pops open and a woman climbs out. I push away the urge to make a joke about women drivers. The joke pops in and out of my head quickly but I keep it to myself. The woman gets stable and surveys the area. She has something big strapped to her back. She watches as packs of freshly turned infected roam the streets killing everyone they meet. She pulls the object from her back. It is an assault rifle. The woman opens fire. She spays bullets in every direction. Unfortunately the Bronco is not bulletproof. Rounds rip through the cabin and engine compartment. She misses our bodies, thank God, but our windshield is gone and I know she has really screwed up our engine. I have played paintball, emphasis on the word played, and I have also been shot with a BB gun. My brother and I thought it would be fun to shoot at each other. We were kids and it was a very stupid idea. Luckily no one was hurt and we were caught by my father immediately.

I have never been shot at by a real gun. It is absolutely terrifying and today it has happened twice. The fear I feel is a very difficult thing to describe. It is an almost unimaginable thing that a little chunk of lead can put a stop to this whole trip. It happens so fast that I don't have much time to dwell on it. She is not trying to shoot us. We are just down range from her real targets. Even with all her wild shots she does manage to cut down a good-sized group of infected. It opens up a little space for us to make our escape. I crank the steering wheel and make a hard left. With the pedal to the metal we leave the crazy woman to her almost certain demise.

I weave down a few blocks and put some distance between the gun-toting lady and us. We have entered into a more industrial area. There are more businesses here than homes. The traffic is much lighter and no one is on the streets. There is an abandoned parking lot ahead of us. I pull into it and yank the emergency brake. We skid to a stop.

"Are you guys okay?" I pivot in my seat to look back at Devon. He rubs his sore face and gives me a thumbs up. He can't even squeak out a "dude" for me. There is a clear as day bullet hole in the seat next to him. Only inches away. Sara has a tight grip on the dash. Her hair has fallen her face. She breathes in her nose and out her mouth. "Are you okay?" I ask again. She raises her hand and holds up her index finger. She still needs a minute. I examine the windshield and there are five holes in it. Another three in the hood. I take a sip of water as I look around the abandoned parking lot. The building is an old strip club. The sign reads "Fuzzy Holes." That's a funny name for a club. On the sign below the name is reads "We fired the ugly one. Come on in!" I like a strip club with a sense of humor. The crack half a smile thinking about if there was an ugly woman working there how long did she shake her nasty udders and dirty mud flaps before she got the axe. Did the guys lay down singles and ask her for change. My half smile quickly goes away and I crank around the rearview mirror. I take a look behind us. The building directly behind us is a gym. The front is smashed open. Busted glass litters the street. I don't think that much of it until I see the beasts that busted open the door. These two look like Schwartzenegger wannabes. Two hundred and fifty pounds each of pure infected muscle rumbles across the street. They are on a collision course with the backend of the Bronco. Fantastic.

Chapter 9

They move really fast for being such big guys. It only takes the two muscle head monsters a few seconds to sprint across the street and into the parking lot. They smash into us like a couple of rhinos. They hit the Bronco so hard that we slide a foot even with the emergency brake on. Their twenty four inch pythons blast through the back window. Devon ducks down. He squeezes his body all the way down to the floorboard. The monsters keep pushing us and the tires grind across the asphalt. The only thing keeping them out of the car is their massive chests and their inability to take turns. Both monsters fight to climb into the same small opening. Meat heads. No way in hell I am stepping out of this car to face them. They would snap me in half and eat me like a protein bar. One of them has his hand on Devon's backpack. He lifts and pulls at him like he weighs nothing.

"Jim?!" Devon holds onto the back of Sara's seat. I drop the emergency brake and put the old V8 into reverse and punch the gas. I back out of the parking lot, across the street and slam into the brick wall of the gym. Their heads are crushed between the wall and the back of the car. These two monsters explode and blood sprays us like a fire hose. The whole inside of the cab feels like it is coated in blood. The tires spin and the engine revs because my foot is still pressed all the way to the floor. I finally let off the gas. I put her back into first and pull away from the wall. They drop out of the back window and fall to the ground. The inside of the windshield is splattered with gunk. I wipe it with my gloved hand so I can see out. I have got to keep us moving. I can't stop. It is horrible every time I do. Devon has a full gallon of blood on him. He runs his hand through his hair to try and squeeze out the excess chunky marinara sauce. Next to him on the seat is a severed jaw. He slides as far away from it as he can.

"Well, this is gross," I try and find a dry spot on my sleeve to rub against my face and clean this crud off. Sara convulses. She is going to puke. She pushes herself as far back into the chair as she can. I finally notice what it is that has sent her over the edge. There is an eyeball in her lap.

"Don't puke!" I beg her. "It is already disgusting in here! Don't add to it," she holds her hand over her mouth trying to keep down the bile. She can't hold it any longer. Puke sprays out between her fingers. I am doused with Sara's hot lunch.

"I'm so sorry," she apologizes. I don't want to look at her. I will lose my lunch too. I am a man in my mid-thirties. I have had my fair share of adult drinks and sometimes the night ends with a little vomit. As a father you also run into puke from time to time when the kids get sick, but that is your kids puke so it is not as bad. I have never had an adult throw up all over me.

I can feel my stomach turn. I don't think I can keep it down. I hate puking. I fight to keep what is in my stomach, in my stomach.

We roll down a little back road that dumps us off at a large intersection. Fifty yards down the street there is an overturned Subaru. It looks like it was hit by another car and is up on its side. It sits in the direction I have to go so I head towards it. I am still fighting my stomach and about to lose the battle. I notice a chunk of hotdog on my sleeve and that is it. I lose it. The streets clear of infected people so I pull over next to the Subaru.

My stomach kicks out every drop of food and water I have had all day. I shake off the extra chunks from Sara. I am dry heaving when I hear the sounds of someone calling for help. It is from the overturned car. I quickly look around to make sure I am not about to be swarmed by a gang of infected. It is clear. It is all empty parking lots and deserted buildings around us. I step a little closer to the overturned car and there is an older woman trapped inside. She stands on her drivers side window and kicks at the windshield. Her car sits in the middle of an intersection. She is trapped.

"Guys, someone's in this car," I reach back into the Bronco and pull out the keys.

"What the hell are you doing?" Sara grabs the sleeve of my coat. I break away from her grip and pull the keys from the ignition.

"We shouldn't stop!" Devon begs. I sprint back to the old lady.

"Oh, thank you!" she is pressed against the glass.

"You're gonna be okay!" I tell her. I search the side of the road and find a big rock. It is the size of a grapefruit.

"Get down!" I yell at her. She squats behind her steering wheel. I chuck the rock as hard as I can. It smacks against the window and the safety glass splinters. The stone falls to the ground. I pick it up and throw it at a different part of the windshield. It smashes the hell out of it but I can't get the rock to punch a hole through the glass. I need something like a bat or crowbar. I kick the glass a few times but I can't get through it. Sara and Devon scream at me from the Bronco, but I can't make out what they are yelling.

"Behind you!" The old lady yells. I turn and there is an infected. It has its hands reached out to grab me. I don't have my spear and I don't have time to pull my machete. It is almost on top of me. The guy was a big heavyset trucker. His flannel shirt is half torn off, exposing a massive wound. The fat from his stomach drips from the open wound and falls to the ground. I put my arm up and catch its teeth with the soccer shin pad that I have strapped to my forearm. He crushes me up against the windshield. Chunks of safety glass fall down the back of my jacket and into my shirt. It bites the pad over and over again, but it has not broken my skin. The pressure from its jaw on my forearm is incredible. I feels like it is about to break my bones. I can't reach my knife and he is so heavy I can't push him off me. He has me pinned between the glass and hood. Crunch! The tip of a knife sticks out from the infected monsters forehead. It falls to the ground. Sara got him with my spear. Thank goodness! When its big body hits the ground a squirt of blood shoots up into the air and splashes her. She lets out a disgusted squeal.

"Is that your first one?" I push myself off the hood.

"No," she hands me the spear. I use it to smash through the glass.

The street we are on snakes south under a set of train tracks and connects with a major street. Around the corner a big rig has emerged. The truck driver has a lead foot and six infected punch and claw at the rig's windows. I give the window a hard front kick.

The hole in her windshield is only a foot wide. Sara pulls at me.

A monster at the driver's side window mauls the man behind the wheel and rips out one of the driver's eyes. He fights for his life, but he can't see. The rig is on a collision course with the Subaru. I kick and kick at it. I reach in to her car and we lock arms. I try and pull her though the window, but she can't fit. Sara pulls at me. We only have seconds to move.

"I'M SORRY!" I yell at the lady. I have to tear my arm away from hers. Sara and I dive for the side of the road. The semi crashes into the car and blows the back of the Subaru apart. Sparks fly as it grinds across the street. The Subaru hits the curb and blasts over a shrub that separates the street from the parking lot. Both the Subaru and the truck crash into a wall of stone. The Subaru explodes into a fireball and seconds after that the semi explodes into an even bigger fireball.

I sit up to readjust my backpack. I can feel the heat of the fire from here. How many more people will I see die today? I went my whole life never seeing anyone die.

"I'm sorry you couldn't save her," she dusts the asphalt from her hands. I stand up and give my back a quick twist to pop my vertebrae. Two creatures crawl out of the fire and I have a strong desire to take my spear and stab the hell out of them. We jog back to the car and watch the two charred and mangled bodies and I wonder about the science behind these things. They can have totally wrecked bodies and keep moving, but one stab to the brain and they are done? On top of that, how the hell does a dead person keep moving?

Doesn't the body need air? Science is not now, and never was, my strong point, but nothing about these things makes any sense.

I don't want to but I get back into the disgusting blood and puke spattered Bronco. I feel deflated and tired. It has only been a little over an hour since that helicopter fell out of the sky, but it feels like I have been running a marathon all day. The thought of seeing this amount of carnage and destruction every day for the rest of my life is absolutely disheartening. When I think about my children witnessing this kind of brutality and loss it is beyond comprehension. Right now I have to put that out of my mind and keep moving. I get the Bronco rolling again.

"No more stops," she spits venom at me.

"Where would you be if I didn't stop," I pull back onto the street.

"No more stops!" she says again. I get the feeling that she is the "last word in every argument" kind of girl. I step on it and head north. The busted out back window moves enough air in here to keep my wrecked nose from only smelling the puke and blood.

"How are you gonna get onto the 205 bridge?" asks Sara.

"We'll take the on-ramp by the airport."

"That's a busy on-ramp. What do you think it's going to be like today?"

"No one's following the letter of the law when it comes to driving, so I'll ride the curb if I have to. I'll drive down the center pedestrian walkway if I have to," I feel some blood drip down onto my upper lip.

"Can you look for some napkins in the glove box?" I ask her. She pops it open and luckily there is a handful. She hands me one. I run it over my upper lip, but the blood keeps coming. She takes one of the napkins and twists it.

"Here," she hands it to me. I jam it up my nostril and grunt out in pain.

"Damn this nose," I whimper. She twists another and I stick it in the other nostril. I look really cool. My nose is all red like Rudolph. It makes Sara giggle a little when I look over at her.

"I don't normally get nosebleeds."

She uses some of the napkins to clean off the blood and puke on her, "What's your wife's name?" she asks. Devon reaches from the backseat for his own handful of napkins to clean himself with.

"Karen. My girls are Valerie and Robin." Saying their names gives me a boost of energy. Sara looks back at Devon and sees that he's dressed like me.

"What's with the gear?"

"We looted some stuff from a sporting goods store," Devon sits up to talk to her.

"They only had the one outfit?" she smirks. I peek a look back at Devon.

"No, this was the best they had...so that's what we took."

"Holy shit!" I yell. A mushroom cloud of black smoke rises in the distance. A few years ago Portland built a shopping center close to the airport. It sits right on the Columbia River. It is called Cascade Station. It has your typical bunch of shopping stores, a Best Buy and Oregon's only Ikea. It is a popular destination in Portland. Right now it is on fire.

Steam begins to creep out from under the hood of the Bronco. The lady with the rifle put a hole in the radiator. Awesome. I am not looking forward to walking, but I will be glad to get the hell out of this chum bucket.

There is a very large field between us and the shopping center and the field is also connected to the freeway. It is only grass out there and it would be a huge shortcut if I drove across the field. I jump the curb and pop up onto the grass. The Bronco tears across the field.

"Where are we going?" Sara has cleaned most of the blood from her face.

"Shortcut," I sound like a cartoon character with my nose all plugged up.

We get up onto a little ridge where we can see the shopping center, and to the west the Portland International Airport. Now we see where the smoke is coming from. A commercial airliner crashed. The plane looks like it hit the edge of the Ikea that sits the farthest east of the shopping center, and then slid across the massive parking lot that connects all of the stores. Half of the fuselage juts out of the Best Buy at the west end of the center. The smell of burning jet fuel fills the air. Along with what I guess is cheap Swedish wood and Chinese electronics. I stop the Bronco at the top of a small ridge so I can get a better look.

"What are you doing?" Sara asks.

"Let's take a look," I pull the keys and I get out of the car. I climb up onto the hood then the roof. We are in the middle of the grass field and there is no one around us so I feel pretty safe out here. The plane is a Boeing 747. The wings of the plane tore off during the crash and one ended up in a place called GolfSmith, the other in a Verizon Wireless store. The fuselage took out hundreds of cars in that parking lot. Most of them are on fire. People run in and out of the stores. Half of them are looting with arms full of discount clothing and cheap electronics. With their cars destroyed I wonder where they are going to put their new stolen property. The others are probably looking for their lost loved ones. Farther to the west is the airport and a few other planes have crashed onto the tarmac. The southern half of the tower that looks over the airport is missing, like it was cut by the world's largest samurai sword.

There is gunfire coming from the airport. A National Guard station is nearby. I hope that they do better against the infected than the police. They have big guns and a bunch of Hummers at that base. I drove by it once on the way to a restaurant and it looked like there were at least thirty Hummers and other transport vehicles there. There are so many dead bodies. Between the airport and Cascade Station there are thousands of people and if they are not dead already they are about to be. This place is going to be crawling with the infected.

To my right is the 205 bridge that crosses the Columbia River into Vancouver and it is full of cars but they are still moving north and south. I scan the rest of the field and it is clear all the way to the 205 freeway. I jump down then I climb back into the Bronco and get it going.

"What's going on?" Devon's face has begun to swell up around his black eye.

"It's biblical, man."

"Oh," he sits back and tries to rest.

"How did the bridge look?" asks Sara.

"Slow, but it's moving," I turn to the right and head east.

We head for a set of train tracks. It is the tracks to the mass-transit system that we call "The Max". Most of the tracks are up on a raised brim of dirt, but there is a spot a little south of the tracks that is suspended. I aim for the suspended part and the Bronco fits under it easy. Steam is really pouring out from under the hood now and the temp gauge rests permanently in the red. The engine has a real nice knocking sound going. It has been a blessing while it lasted.

"What's that noise?" Devon sits back up.

"We've overheated. It's probably blown the head gasket," I tell him. In my early twenties I owned a Mercedes-Benz. It was their starting model but it was still a Benz. I loved that car. It had leather seats, moon roof and power everything. At the time I didn't have a very good job and I was not making enough money. I could not take care of it and I would forget to change the oil or add coolant. I would eventually overheat the engine, so I know exactly what those sounds are.

"What does that mean?" Devon's head is right between ours.

"We don't have much engine left," says Sara.

"Really?" his voice cracks.

"Yep," I concur.

The southbound lane of the freeway is pretty clear. A lot of people are like me. They live in Vancouver but work in Portland. The northbound lane on the other hand is packed. It is slower than a normal five o'clock rush hour. Vehicles are spread across the four lanes and into the two emergency lanes. They are bumper to bumper all the way up the bridge. It is a two-mile long bridge from Oregon into Washington. Closer to the Oregon side is Government Island, a large stretch of land in the middle of the Columbia River. It is covered with trees and the only way to get to it is by boat. I have lived here all my life and I have never set foot onto that island. I don't know anyone with a boat and I have never had the means to own one myself. Plus the idea of spending all day on an island that has nothing on it but trees and no toilets doesn't sound like a party to me. After Government Island the bridge takes a steep climb over the water to allow ships to pass below without needing a drawbridge. The bridge has four lanes in both directions and a small strip down the center for people to walk or ride bikes. There is no way this car will make it up the bridge in this traffic without overheating and stalling out.

"What are we gonna do?" Devon pats me on the shoulder. I pull the Bronco onto the southbound lane and head north. Cars zip by.

"What are you doing?" asks Sara.

"I'm gonna drive up the wrong side of the bridge," I punch the gas. I stay in the emergency lane as cars race past me at over eighty miles an hour.

"This is outrageous!" Devon yells.

"We won't make it otherwise." Cars honk their horns at us as they pass. We approach the first exit off of 205, the one you would take to get to the airport. No one is going that way so we race past it.

We are now on the bridge. I hug tight to the concrete wall that lines the edge of the bridge. It is working. We are going to make it across. I sigh in relief.

"HOLY FUCK!" cries Sara. I try and see what she is looking at. It is another jumbo jet and it is headed right for the bridge. It drops out of the sky at three hundred miles an hour. The plane hits the bridge square on. Its left wing has dipped lower than the bridge so it cuts deep into the east side of 205. Then its body slams down onto the asphalt. It crushes all of the cars across all eight lanes. For a few terrible seconds time slows down. The plane explodes in a colossal fireball that engulfs everything in a fifty-yard radius. We are only a hundred yards away. The sound of the crash and the explosion is deafening. Even through the windshield I can feel the extreme heat. I slam down on the brakes. A car drives out of the fireball. Its front right tire has blown out and the driver loses control. The car is going to hit us head on. I swerve out onto the freeway to avoid it. The car hits us and the Bronco spins. A truck hits our front end; we spin back around and start to roll. We smash around inside. My face is peppered with broken glass. My spear smacks around between the two front seats. Metal crushing, tires screeching and a hundred tons of concrete crumbling under the weight of the plane. I have never heard anything like it. This is it. We are dead. I know it. My head hits the steering wheel and everything goes black.

Chapter 10

I jerk awake. I am upside down in the Bronco. Devon lies on the ceiling knocked out. Sara is unconscious next to me in the passengers seat. I reach up and feel the gash on my forehead. I thought my head hurt before, now it is killing me. Between my broken nose, my neck injury from my first car crash, the back of my head smacking into the car during the fight with the blonde guy and now this deep cut on my forehead, I feel like quitting. There are screams in the distance outside of the Bronco. The reality of what happened and where I am sets in.

I have got to get out of here. We need to keep moving. I fight to get my seat belt undone, but I can't get the button to release. I pull the knife from my hip and cut the safety belt. I fall down onto my head. Ouch. My hair mops up the blood on the ceiling as I fall on my neck and shoulder. My neck and ear grind into the glass shards. I twist and pivot and I get to my butt and sit upright. I take a drag of water from my pack then reach out and shake Devon.

"Wake up!"

His eyes pop open. Waking up Devon reminds me of when my Dad would wake me and my brother up to get ready for school. I was ten at the time so Don would have been eight. It would be early in the morning, dark outside and Dad would open our bedroom door and turn on the light. "Get up!" is all he would say. It worked every time.

"What happened?" Devon sits up quickly and then feels how much his body hurts. He lets out a groan that wakes up Sara. She screams right away.

"You're okay. Calm down," I tell her. I hold her as I undo her seat belt. It releases and she falls down into my arms and I help her get upright. Devon makes his way to the busted out back window. I let Sara go first and she follows him. I find my spear but the blade is buried deep into the dash. I have to work it back and forth to get it free. I slide out the back of the Bronco and get to my feet.

When I get upright I give my body a good once over to see if anything is broken. I pull the blood soaked napkins from my nose and toss them to the ground. I look around. The bridge is gone. The plane crashed south of Government Island and took out a hundred and fifty foot chunk. The full width of the bridge is gone. I walk out to the edge and Devon and Sara follow me. We stand about ten feet from the crumbling asphalt and concrete. We are thirty feet in the air and there is no way across. The plane sticks partially out of the water of the Columbia River. I pull my phone from my pocket, kick it on and realized we were knocked out for a couple minutes.

"What should we do?" asks Devon.

"I don't know," I answer grimly.

"Should we try and get a boat?" asks Sara. I look back down the bridge into Portland. There is a massive horde about a thousand strong, moving quickly up the 205 freeway killing everyone, and adding to their numbers. I swipe my phone on and dial Karen. It rings a few times before she picks up.

"Jim, thank God! Are you okay? Where are you?" she is panicked. I have never heard her like this before. I don't want to make it worse so I have to choose my words carefully.

"Karen, I'm fine. I'm on the 205 bridge. Are you and the girls safe?"

"Yes. We are okay." I hear it in her voice. She chooses her words to not upset me. We do this when I know my paycheck is going to be light or if she has spent too much money that month. We try and dance around it so that we don't scare each other.

"Jim, bro!" Devon gets his spear ready to fight the growing horde.

"Baby, I'm coming home. You kiss those girls for me and tell them that Dad's on his way," tears build up in my eyes.

"I will. Jim, please hurry home. People are going...nuts." The infected are only fifty feet away and moving fast. Devon and Sara are freaked out and want me off the phone.

"I love you so much. I'll see you soon."

"I love you too." I hang up the phone and slide it back into my pocket.

I take off and sprint as hard as I can. Like I said I hate heights and the only thing worse than being up on something high is jumping off of it. This is much higher than the jump we did onto the van. As I approach the broken edge of the bridge all of my fear and anxiety about heights bubbles up into my brain. It tries so hard to talk me out of this. It lists everything that can go wrong. Broken bones and drowning are the top two that my brain keeps repeating.

I jump, holding my spear tight as I brace for the impact of the water. It feels like forever. My body wants to shit itself. I am not sure about the best way to land. I keep my legs aiming straight down. I know I don't want to land on my back or my face. I clench every hole I have. Then I hit the water. It is much colder than I thought it would be. I hit so hard that my sinuses are blasted with what feels like five gallons of liquid. I swim for the surface. Being fully dressed with a backpack on and a spear in one hand, I start to panic. I am not a strong swimmer. This climb to the surface pushes me to the breaking point. It takes forever for me to breach, I am going to run out of air.

I gasp a lungful when my head breaks the surface. Seconds later Devon and Sara hit the water next to me. I swim for Government Island. Sara and Devon have surfaced and they follow me to the island. The current in the Columbia River is strong. It pulls me quickly to the west. I live on the east side of Vancouver. I have to get to this island. If I miss it then it will be a very long swim across the river. At the rate the water carries me I might end up miles downriver and have to walk back that much farther. So I fight and push myself across. It takes everything I have to keep going. My nose kills me every time I take a breath in. My legs and arms feel numb. This water is less than sixty degrees and it is murky. You can't see more than two feet into it.

"Damn, this water is movin' fast," Devon fights hard to make it.

A wave smacks Sara in the face. "I hate this river," she coughs and spits.

The thought occurs to me that if someone drowned on the plane they will turn and come back as an infected. When I was a kid swimming at a lake called Round Butte, I had the fear that something was going to grab my leg and pull me down under the water. I think I saw it in one of the *Friday The 13th* movies. Jason reaches up from the water and pulls his victim to their death. It is all I can think about. A hundred Jasons grabbing my ankle and pulling me under. I also have an irrational fear of freshwater sharks so this is the most nightmarish swim of my life. I am halfway to the island when I hear it. I look back at the bridge and the infected are falling from the edge. My nightmare has come true; the monsters are in the water. I don't see any of them surface, but they don't need air. I push hard until I get my feet to solid ground.

I climb out of the water and up onto the small sandy beach. We are a couple hundred yards down the river from the bridge, but we made it. The island is shaped like a giant joint if you looked down on it from a plane. We landed at one tip of the joint. We need to walk to the other tip before climbing back into the water. If we don't we will end up miles away from my family. Our apartment sits east about four miles from the 205 freeway we jumped from. I lay on the sand trying to catch my breath. The only thing worse than running is running soaking wet. Even though I am drenched I take another drink of water. Devon and Sara join me on the beach. They are zonked.

"Come on guys. We have to keep moving," I don't sound very convincing when I say it.

Devon holds up two fingers, "Two minutes bro." My kids pull this same move when we have to leave some place and they are having fun.

"We don't have two minutes. You saw them fall into the water. They could climb out onto the beach any second. Let's move," I hold out my hand and help Devon up first, then Sara. We start jogging in the sand.

"We need to get to the north side of the island," I say over my shoulder to them. To get to the north side we will have to cross through the forest. I see the start of a trail so I head in that direction.

The infected continue to fall off the edge of the bridge, but they don't pop back up to the surface. They must sink straight to the bottom. Maybe they won't be a problem. The current is so fast I hope the river takes them all the way to the ocean.

"When we get to the north side, then what?" asks Devon.

"We swim," I huff and puff up the sandy beach.

"It's an even further swim to Washington," Sara chimes in.

"I know it. We don't have a ton of options," I have to stop talking as I run or I am going to pass out.

We get to the opening of the trail and I slow down. My eyes adjust to the dark. If this was a normal day and I walked through woods like this I would be fine, but after everything I have seen today, these woods are absolutely terrifying. It is so dark and hard to see. I lead the way, Sara follows and Devon watches our backs.

"It's spooky," Devon whispers.

When I was twelve we moved north of Battle Ground, Washington. It was five acres of forest out in the middle of nowhere. We had deer in the front yard and stars in the sky at night. "God's country," as my Dad called it. I lived out there for eight years, but I would not call myself an outdoor man or a country boy. I don't know how to hunt nor fish, we just shopped at the local Safeway. I can't call this the deep woods, the city is behind me and Vancouver is peeking out from the trees ahead.

The trail we jog on is worn and well kept. I can't hear anything other than the sound of our feet and heavy breathing. I am glad to see Devon and Sara huff and puff as badly as I am. My sopping wet clothes seem to have added twenty pounds to me and these top of the line boots rub my feet raw. We are close to the north beach now. The last half of the 205 bridge is right ahead of us. It looks so high up in the air from down here. The bridge touches down onto the island for a quarter mile then rises up high above the Columbia River.

We hit the beach and I have to slow down. I promised myself that I would take up running for exercise, but I never did. Now I am paying for it.

"Hold up guys," I slow to a fast walk. "My nose is killing me," I blame the nose but it is my whole body that's screaming "NO." We are close to the bridge. There are screams and commotion up on the bridge. I can't make it out. I hear the moan of the infected. There is a chain-link fence that separates the freeway from the island and it wraps around all four sides of the bridge. A small horde is smashed up against the fence. We need to keep moving, so I pick up the pace.

They have spotted us and it gets them all riled up. They shuffle down the fence and climb over the concrete barrier that lines the bridge. Their bodies fall and tumble onto the island. One after another they fall on top of each other. A few of them land on their feet and they move right for us. The fence dips under the bridge. It is designed to keep people off the island. Right now it gives us a few more seconds to get past them. The fence is topped with razor wire but they do not try to climb over. They push and bite at the metal barrier. We run under the bridge and are shaded from the hot sun. More and more infected pour down onto the island. The fence is about to give. I stop and face the monsters. I stab at them. I demolish a dead housewife's face.

"What are you doing?!" Sara yells.

"This fence is gonna give! We need to take down a few of them so it will hold!" Devon follows me and starts stabbing away with his spear. Sara pulls the machete from Devon's hip. Over and over we stab through the fence. The last time I saw real human brains outside of the skull was in my sophomore biology class. Today I have seen dozens of shattered skulls with brains leaking out of them. I am so ready for this day to be over.

At the east end of the bridge stands thirty monsters. Pushing against the barrier.

"Come on!" I sprint for the other end of the fence. A big one, a full on "Walmart Mom" as wide as she is tall falls over the concrete divider and crash-lands into the fence. I quickly take out another five monsters, but her weight was enough to pop the fence off its post. They spill out onto the sand under the bridge. I take out a few more and keep running. I slash and stab at them. Blood, guts and brains drop to the sand. Devon and Sara take down four or five each, but we can't kill them fast enough. They are about to surround us. We have to go now.

"RUN!" I scream. We take off down the beach away from the bridge. There are too many. If we stay and fight they will easily overwhelm us.

We get two hundred feet away from the bridge when I smell it. Cow shit. Why do I smell cow shit out here? We run around the little bit of woods and the island opens up to a pasture. There are a few hundred cows hanging out eating grass. We run into the pasture and it freaks out some of the bovine. They take off and run into each other. Someone yells at us and it is not one of the infected. It is coming from the cows. There is a man out in the middle of the herd. He is tending to one of the animals. As we get closer, the sea of cows parts and we see the man in his late fifties next to a four-wheeler. It is the kind of knobby-wheeled thing you would use on a ranch.

"What the hell are you people doing?" he readjusts his baseball cap.

"Start the four-wheeler," I shriek at him.

"You people shouldn't be here!" he catches a full view of the disgusting army of the dead that are on our heels. The horde splits up and chase after the cows. Devon, Sara and I reach the four-wheeler.

"Come on man!" Devon says to the farmer. He climbs onto his ride and the three of us jump up onto the racks. The guy turns a key and hits the ignition. He punches the gas and the tires spin out as we take off. The infected chow down on a few of the cows. They swarm them, tearing at their flesh. One cow trips on a dead person, falls to its side and they tear into it. Some of the other livestock get away but suffer a few bites from the infected. The farmer heads for a small house and barn that sits at the end of the pasture. The horde has forgotten about us and is focused on this easy prey.

The farmer pulls into the barn and kills the vehicle's engine. He hops off and runs for one of the barn doors. Devon and I run over to the other door and pull it closed.

"What in God's name is going on? The girls have been going crazy for the last hour. I see smoke in the sky. I heard the God-awful noise. It sounded like a plane crash," the farmer pulls off his baseball cap and wipes the sweat from his forehead. He stares at us waiting for some kind of rational answer.

"I don't know what to tell you. It doesn't make a lot of sense. There is a horrible infection spreading quickly," I tell him. He snaps his cap back on.

"The noise and the smoke?" he asks.

"A few planes have crashed. They took out the bridge, Cascade Station and the airport. Is there a way out of here?" I press. I notice Devon is right behind me. He shadows every move I make. I didn't notice it before now.

"Yeah. Back door."

"Do you have a boat?" asks Sara. "You want to go out there?" he drops his hands onto his hips in disbelief.

"Hey," I put my hand out and he shakes it on instinct. "My name's Jim, what's yours?"

"Bob," he says.

"Bob, we can't hang around here. Those things will find a way in or they'll surround us and we'll never get out," he does not believe me. "Bob, we gotta move now. If this is happening everywhere, then there's no rescue. Do you have a boat off this island?" I let go of his hand. He looks the three of us over and makes eye contact with each of us. It sinks in. How could we possibly make this up? He nods his head.

"I got a boat tied up at the dock. It's north of here. Keys are in the house."

"Okay. Lead the way."

Bob heads to the back door of the barn. He slowly pops it open and peeks outside. The coast is clear so we follow him out. He walks quickly.

"Let's pick up the pace," I jog past him. Out in the pasture, four dead cows are on the ground. The infected chase after the rest of the animals. I hope they stay occupied with the herd and give us time to get off this island.

We get to the front door and Bob unlocks it. We slide through the door and into the small entryway. Bob locks the door behind us. I keep watch at the window as he hunts for his keys.

"I got a rifle. Should I grab it?"

"Whatever you want. Just move fast," says Sara.

"I recommend a blade," I tell him. Bob finds the keys to the boat in a drawer.

"I'm going to grab my rifle. Where are we going?" Bob goes to get his gun.

"Vancouver," says Sara. Bob returns from down the hall and loads a handful of rounds into the old Winchester.

"Why?"

"My family. Keep it down," I whisper. The infected are close.

"I can drop you off on the shore, but I'm heading upriver. I got a cabin in Stevenson."

Out in the pasture something horrible has happened. I thought this was a people disease, but I was wrong. One of the cattle has turned and it is pissed off.

Devon looks over my shoulder outside. "What the hell?" he whispers to me. Bob fills a backpack with canned food. His rifle is slung over his forearm. He turns quickly and the barrel of the gun hits a quart jar full of coins. The jar slides off the kitchen counter and crashes to the ground. Glass and coins hit the hardwood floor and the jar explodes. It could not have been louder. The infected out in the pasture hear the noise and move for us.

"Oops," Bob says as he slings his pack up onto his shoulder.

The cow charges at the house as Bob opens the front door. Its ribs are exposed and it is missing its jaw. Bob raises his rifle and fires, hitting its chest. The round does nothing but alert all of the infected to our location.

"Hit them in the head!" Sara roars. He fires another round and hits the neck. The cow moves so fast, faster than the rest of the infected. Two more beasts have turned and head our way. The first one is at the door. Bob slams it shut. The animal blasts the front door off its hinges. Its head and neck stick into the living room, but it is too wide. The doorway stops it. Bob fires another round and misses completely. Its head rears up and down as it fights to get inside. I stab at it and slice off an ear. Devon takes his spear and slices downward into its neck. He cuts the head halfway off. I hit it the same way on my side and the damn thing's head falls to the floor. Gallon after gallon of cow blood pour out of its neck. The body drops onto the porch. The eyes and tongue move in the severed head. It is still alive. Sara forces her machete down into its brain. That does it.

Four infected humans climb over the dead cow's body. Bob shoots one in the head and I slice at another. Another turned cow crashes through the big front window, but it gets high centered on the windowsill. We back into the kitchen. The infected smash through the windows and front door. Their blood soaked mouths snap closed. Bob fires until his rifle clicks empty. If we do not move we will be surrounded. I do not want to face a turned cow in the open.

We move further into the kitchen. I see a full bottle of whiskey on the counter. I pull open a drawer next to the sink and find a dish rag. I grab the whiskey and jam the rag into the mouth of the bottle.

"That won't kill them!" hollers Devon. I pull the Zippo from my pocket and light the rag.

"I know, but it'll slow them down," I give the rag a few seconds and then I throw it into the living room. It hits one of the infected and bounces off and rolls to the floor. Nothing happens. "What the hell?" I groan.

"Now what?" Sara looks around the kitchen for something else to throw, but there is nothing. One of the infected steps on the flaming rag and it snuffs out the fire. Bob franticly reloads his rifle. Devon takes down one that entered the kitchen. A turned cow has somehow shoved itself through the window and it smashes around the living room. I pass a bookshelf as we leave the kitchen. I stick the blade of my spear between it and the wall and give my spear a good hard push. The bookshelf tips over and comes crashing down onto the kitchen counter.

"Let's move our asses!" Bob leads us to the bedroom and slides open the window. It is barely big enough for us to climb out. This side of the house is on a slope so it is a ten-foot drop out the window. Devon goes first. He sits on the sill and dangles his legs out. When he hits the ground he slides down the grassy hill and comes to a stop fifteen feet away from the house.

"I made it!" he calls up to us. Two of the infected have climbed over the bookshelf. I stab them right away. Sara jumps next and makes it. Bob climbs up into the window. As he fights to get his legs out I take down a couple more freaks. The livestock or I guess, the deadstock now, smash through the house. I am back to back with Bob as he readies himself. Four more infected stumble into the bedroom and I take down the first one. My spear is stuck in its face and the three others are right on top of me. I rip the spear out and swing it hard and it slices off the head of one of them. The last two have their hands on me so I use the shaft of the spear to block them. I catch them under their arms and put the shaft right up into their sternums. They force me back and I knock Bob out of the window. When he hits the ground the rifle goes off.

"AHHHAH! SON OF A BITCH!" Bob screeches in pain.

The infected push my head and shoulders out the open window. The spear is caught against the frame and the wall. It stops them. They can't reach me with their blood caked mouths. I look down at Bob and he has shot himself in the leg. The infected put all of their weight on me. The spear bows under the pressure. I am stuck halfway in and out of this window. I let go of the spear and pull the knife from my hip. I stab the one on my right and its body falls to the floor. I shove against the last one. I am able to get the handle of the spear out the window and I begin to fall. It is ten feet to the ground and I am going to land hard on my back. Awesome.

Chapter 11

The fall was not as bad as I thought it was going to be. The impact itself was not what hurt. The grass was soft and I hit it at a good angle and I slid easily down the hill on my back. What hurt was the sharp rock that sliced down the side of my right calf. It tore through my new pants and left a three inch gash.

When I was twenty years old, I thought it was time I got a tattoo. So I put a Chinese symbol on my right leg. It was the symbol for money or so I was told. I could be a walking advertisement for Chinese laundry detergent. I do not really know. It sits a couple inches above my ankle and it's the only tattoo on my body. I never liked it. A couple years ago I met a lady in her mid fifties and she had almost the exact tattoo in the same spot. After that I really hated my ink. The rock cut it in two. Slit it right down the middle. Now if I live through all of this I will have an ugly scar to go with my bad tattoo. I get to the bottom of the hill and crash into Bob. He lets out a squeal.

"We've got to stop the bleeding!" Sara holds his wound.

"With what?" Devon is in a panic.

"I don't know," she walks over to Bob then cuts and tears off a strip from his t-shirt and pulls off his belt. She shoves the rag onto the wound, wraps the belt around his leg then pulls the belt tight and ties it off. Up in the window an infected climbs out after us. It falls and tumbles down the hill. I roll to my stomach and get to my knees. It falls head over heels. I ready myself, get my spear up and aim it at the monster. I stab him right in the chest and the force of it jams my handle down deep into the dirt behind me. My spear is stuck in the ground and its chest. Sara gets to her feet and gives it a chop to the head. Its skull splits in half. Another infected falls out the window and lands on Bob. Devon moves quickly and stabs down into the back of its head, but in his haste he did not see Bob's leg was underneath. Devon's spear goes right into Bob's thigh. Black blood pours into Bob's open wound. He lets out a high pitch screech. Devon pulls out the spear and kicks the infected off of Bob and sees what he has done.

"Oh, God! I'm so sorry!" Devon puts pressure on the new wound.

"YOU IDIOT!" Bob shouts through clenched teeth. I slowly get to my feet and test my leg. It hurts like hell but I can at least walk. Bob has shot off a chunk of his calf. It looks like Devon hit an artery. Bob's blood pumps onto the grass. It seeps through Devon's fingers. Behind the house is another forest, thick with trees. I do not want to face one of those turned cows out here in the open, it would run right over us. Bob's face has gone white. He does not have long.

"Get him up!" I lift up Bob's arm and pull him to his feet. Devon gets under his other arm. It is tough to hold both him and my spear.

"I can't believe I stabbed him!"

"It was an accident! We gotta move. Head for the forest."

"Should we leave him? We can't fix him now!" Sara jumps out ahead of us for the woods.

"You know where his boat is docked?"

We move as fast as we can for the edge of the woods. I hope that we can get there and maybe they will lose track of us. We move slower than the infected as we cross the field. It is a hundred yards until we hit the trees. Carrying Bob like this reminds me of high school wrestling. Every year during Christmas break it was a tradition to run up Tukes Mountain. It is more of a super tall hill than a mountain. It sat a couple miles from the high school and was paved all the way to the top. You had to do the run if you wanted to letter in wrestling. On top of that you got your name on the wall with your finish time. They had over ten years worth of names up there by the time I entered high school so it was a badge of honor to run it. We ran it once on Christmas Eve morning. It was freezing out and my lungs burned with every breath. The run started at the high school, then down Main Street and up the hill. The thing that reminds me of this horrible walk is you had to make the run with one of your teammates on your back. You would pair up with someone in your weight class and run as fast as you can, for as long as you can, then you would switch. You would think being carried would be easy, but it was not. You still had to engage your arms and legs to help stay on their back. I can't remember how long it took to get to the top of the mountain but it felt like forever. As I drag Bob I wonder when is it my turn to be carried?

I am not in the same kind of shape I was in high school and Bob is not a hundred and forty pound teenager. We are only thirty yards from the tree line when I hear it. I look over my shoulder. One of the turned cows has fallen out of Bob's window and crash-landed down the hill behind the house. It must have broken a limb in the fall because it drags its rear leg as it limps toward us.

"Push it!" Devon and I pick up the pace. We are so close to the woods. Another cow and a few more infected humans fall down the hill behind us. Shit.

The woods slow us down even more. The underbrush is so thick we are moving at a snails pace.

"Bob, is there a faster way to the boat?" Sara chops at the brush with her machete. He looks up and glances around. Then motions to our right. We head in that direction. The three legged cow smashes through the woods behind us. The underbrush is no problem for her. The forest is so thick I can't see it but I know the beast is there.

It is a slog. Every step we take is a fight. I hurt all over. My clothes are still wet and Bob's dead weight dragging me down.

My mind flashes to *Young Frankenstein* when Gene Wilder digs up the dead body with Igor and he says "What a filthy job." Igor- "Could be worse." Frankenstein- "How?" Igor- "Could be raining." Lightning cracks and down comes the rain. It is a great scene. Made me laugh even as a child. *Can't get any worse* I think to myself. Then Bob pukes blood on me. That is twice in one day. So it did technically get a little worse, but at least it is not raining. My wife is always telling me me stop complaining. She says I am always complaining about this pain or that pain and most of the time she is right. After ten years of marriage you can run out of stuff to talk about and my back hurting badly from a heavy workout seems like a good topic. After a long hard walk we get to a small path.

"Bob! Which way?"

No response.

"BOB!"

His head pops up and he looks up and down the path. He is fading. We don't have much time. He will turn from the sick blood that poured into his leg or bleed to death and try and bite my ear off. I reach into his front pocket and dig out the keys to the boat. Bob nods to the left towards north. Down the path we go. Something smashes around the forest. It is the three-legged beast. On the right side of the path there is a large log, three and a half feet high and it has been down for a long time. It is covered in moss and rotted from the elements.

"Get down," I mouth to the group. We duck behind the old dead growth. It completely hides us from what is about to come. The monster emerges. Step, step, step, drag. I fight to get my breath under control. I do not want it to hear me. It creeps down the gravel road behind us. We don't move. We don't breathe. It doesn't know we are here. Bob has passed out, but his leg twitches. He is about to change. I lean over and put my forearm across his legs to stop the noise. I don't think it heard us. I pull out my knife and get ready to take Bob out. I keep the tip of the blade under his chin. His body shakes. I know that stupid cow heard us. I force the knife up into Bob's brain. I pull it out and wipe the blood off on Bob's shirt.

It is silent for a few seconds, but then a set of hooves slam down onto the log. Out of the three of us, I scream the loudest. We crab walk and twist away from the creature while trying to stab it. It tries to climb over the tree, but its busted leg makes it impossible.

We slash at its face. Large chunks of meat fall from its skull. Devon lands the killshot and its massive body falls dead onto the log. He pulls the spear from its big head and wipes the blood off on its cowhide. I love this kid. What a funny thing to copy. No time to celebrate, we have got to move. I give Bob's body one last look. Another person I could not save. The bodies are piling up in the "I could not save" pile. I can't dwell on it but every time it happens I feel a deep sorrow. I make sure I have his boat keys and we are off.

I sprint back out onto the path. The path opens onto a beautiful view of my city. Vancouver is right there. It looks so close, like I can reach out and touch it. I wipe the sweat from my eyes and take another look. A dark cloud looms above the city. Smoke from fires burning out of control all over the city. My heart aches at the thought of my family burning to death. By boat it is a two-minute ride across the river. If we swim it will take over an hour. The path widens even farther. The dock is right ahead of us. There is a small fishing boat and a bigger ski boat tied to the dock. I hope we get to ride in the big boat.

Everything is clear on the beach. No infected and no devil cows. Our boots smack down onto the aluminum metal dock. It echoes loudly giving away our position to any infected in the area. We get to the last leg of the dock. I am ten feet from the large boat when a rough looking man in his sixties steps out from its cabin. He holds a revolver in his hand and draws down on us as we come to an abrupt stop. Our hands go up in the air. I wish I had a gun on me. His face says it all.

He is freaked out and liable to do something stupid.

"I'm looking for my brother!" he has similar features to Bob only older. He steps farther from the cabin and onto the back part of his boat.

"Have you seen him? His name is Bob. I came to get him when I saw the news."

"We've seen him. I'm sorry, we tried to help," I plead.

"Is that his blood?!"

"Some of it. He'd taken a bad fall and shot himself," no need to tell him about what Devon and I did. Tears form in his eyes. He steps out onto the dock.

"Take me to him! Now!"

"I'm sorry, but he's gone. The island's covered with the infected. It's not safe."

He pulls back the hammer on his gun. "Take me to his body!" tears trickle down the deep cracks in his face and he spits when he talks.

"I've got a brother too and I don't know what's happened to him either. I'm very sorry for your loss-"

"He's down that path about two hundred yards and behind a large log. Please let us go!" blurts out Devon.

"Sir, your brother saved us and we did everything we could for him, but right now we have to get off this island," a small horde steps out of the woods. Perfect timing. They pour out onto the beach. "This place is overrun. We have to get out of here. Please. My name is Jim," I hold out my hand to shake his. It worked with his brother; I hope it will work for him.

"Get out of my way!"

He pushes past us and runs down the dock. We watch him as he unloads his revolver into the first infected reaching the dock. One of the six shots hits it in the head and it falls face first to the aluminum grate. He quickly reloads his gun, much faster than I could reload a gun like that.

"Let's fire this baby up and get of this shitty island," Sara heads for the small boat. She is right. We should leave. I don't know the man nor owe him anything, but I feel guilty. I know how much I would miss my brother if something happened to him. My brother, Don, is a gun nut and works from home. If anyone is doing okay during all this ridiculous shit, it is him. Sara is in the boat and Devon has already undone the first mooring rope. Bob's brother empties his revolver into another infected and it drops dead. I step off the dock and down into the boat. I turn the ignition. Nothing happens. The engine is dead maybe the battery, I have no idea. I look over the rest of the controls and there is nothing to it. No other buttons or a choke to pull, only the ignition and the throttle. I turn the key again. Nothing.

Bob's brother has gunned down another one. He has it figured out. Headshots are what it takes. He took down the whole small horde, all ten. It was impressive.

"Battery's dead!" he reloads his gun. "You want off this island? You gotta help me get my brother!"

Damn it. My choices are to say, "*screw you*", jump into the Columbia River, lose an hour and be exhausted or spend ten minutes and help him drag his brother off this deadly island. Another choice is I wait for him to drop his guard, kill him then take the keys off his dead body. What is wrong with me? I shake off that thought.

"Come on," I step off the boat and back up onto the dock.

"Let's kill him and take the keys," Sara says quietly. I guess the thought of murder is contagious. In a few short hours we go from trying to save everyone to lets kill them if they get in my way.

"No, let's go get Bob," I say, frustrated. Sara and Devon climb out and follow me. I get to the end of the dock and step over the pile of bodies.

"What's your name?"

"Frank,"

"Frank, these things are attracted to sound. So keep the shots to a minimum. If we come across one or two let us take care of it."

"Alright."

"We'll help you get your brother and then you drop us off on the Vancouver side of the river. Deal?" I hold out my hand again. This time he takes it and we shake.

"Deal."

It is like shaking hands with a stone giant. His bear paw of a hand engulfs and crushes mine. He must wash them with sandpaper. Devon and Sara cross over the dead bodies. They don't try and hide how pissed they are at me. Frank leads us off the beach.

We move quickly back into the woods. One of the infected tumbles out onto the gravel and falls at Devon's feet. He yells at the top of his lungs. I don't blame him. The thing is the most mangled looking ex-human I have ever seen. It was only held together by the tattered blood soaked clothes on its back. I think it was a female. It is hard to tell. It looks like it was shot through a de-barking machine. It oozes black slime from every part of its body. It is a horror and it stinks. It is not a rotted meat smell. More of a port-a-potty in the hot sun kind of stink. Devon quickly puts the thing out of its misery. Frank dry heaves and his eyes flutter like he is going to pass out.

"Stop looking at it," I turn him away from the dead body. "We're almost there," I have to pull Frank along.

"Goddamn, what happened to these people?" he spits a little.

"We don't know. Some kind of infection."

Two more appear behind us on the path. They are so quiet. I don't hear them behind us until they are only a few feet away. I take one out fast and easy with a hard stab to its face. Sara swings her machete down onto the other one's head. Her blade gets stuck in the skull. As it falls to the ground it takes the machete with it. She tries to pull it out but it is stuck. Devon puts his boot on the dead man's head and wrenches the blade out. He hands it back to her and their hands touch. He gives her a cheesy grin. *Kids.* We are almost there. Frank stares at the dead cow across the log.

"What's this?"

"Animals can catch it too." I slow down. Something moves on the other side of the log. We step off the path and get around the end of the tree. Four infected monsters are eating Bob's body. They have chewed up his hands, face and one has disemboweled him. It scoops his guts into its mouth. Frank guns them down in a flash. He kneels down and pushes the dead bodies off of his brother. Tears stream down his cheeks. He sobs as he pulls his dead brother's body close to his. My heart goes out to him.

"Come on," I touch Frank's shoulder. He shrugs me off.

"We need to get back to the boat," whispers Devon. Sara moves a little closer. Her grip tightens on her machete. She moves in behind Frank.

"Devon, Sara, keep an eye out."

"Fine," she grits her teeth.

They stand guard at the end of the log. I slide my spear down between my back and the pack I am wearing.

"Frank," he pulls away from his brother. We lay the body down on the ground. He holsters his revolver. I hook my arms under Bob's and Frank hooks under his legs.

"Devon, you lead the way. Sara, watch our backs."

We truck down the gravel path and run as fast as we can. Bob was six foot two and two hundred and thirty pounds. I struggle to carry the body this way. Frank is a tough old bird. I can't imagine carrying my dead brother like this. I would have a mental breakdown. Frank runs hard and seems like he could move faster if he wanted to. I am slowing him down. An infected pops out of the woods in front of us. Devon cuts him down without breaking his stride. A few more are behind us. It is incredible how they can magically appear sometimes. You look away for a second and then when you look back there are two of them. You would think I would be out of adrenaline but it keeps pumping through me. We move fast enough that they can't run us down from behind.

We are back out onto the beach and twenty infected turn to greet us. They mill around at the end of the dock, close to Frank's pile of dead bodies. It is too many for Devon and Sara to take on by themselves and there is no way around them.

"We have to put him down." He nods his head and we carefully lay Bob on the sand. The second Frank lets go of his brother's body he draws his pistol and hits two infected dead center of their foreheads. He made that shot from thirty feet away. My arms are shaky from carrying his brother. I fight to get my spear from my backpack. Frank pulls shells from his pocket, reloads and guns down another six monsters within a few seconds. It is phenomenal. I run over to the remaining infected and the three of us hack, slash and stab them to pieces. Frank reloads. I cut down an infected and look back at Frank.

"Behind you!"

Frank turns and there are fifty creatures both human and bovine, stepping from the tree line. Frank grabs Bob by the wrist. He drags the body across the sand as he shoots another six. Sara takes the head off the last one by the dock. I sprint to Frank's side and grab Bob's other arm. We pull with all of our strength. Frank can't reload, so he holsters his gun and uses both hands to pull. There is a pile of bodies on the dock. Sara and Devon kick the bodies off the grates to clear a path. The monsters gain on us. We hit the dock and keep moving.

"UNTIE THE BOAT!"

The kids race to the boat and unhook the two lines. The infected stream onto the dock, they knock each other off into the water. They are closing the gap. At the pace we are moving they will get to us before we can get Bob's body onto the boat. I don't want this to happen again. I couldn't save my manager and friend, Bill. I couldn't save Bob, but I can help Frank not leave his brother behind. I dig deep inside myself and I pull harder. Tears well up in my eyes thinking about Bill and Sam. I convince myself that if I can get Bob's body into the boat and not leave him for these monsters to feed upon, it will put a notch on my win column. So much of today has been a loss. I need this win. We finally reach the boat.

"Devon, help him!" I let go of Bob and Devon takes over. I stand by the end of the boat and face the shuffling horde. I stab at their ugly twisted faces. I hit them hard enough to knock some of them backwards and that slows them down. They stumble and trip over the bodies. I will not let them get passed me. Devon and Frank pull Bob's body down onto the back of the boat. Frank hands Devon the keys to the boat.

"Fire it up, boy!" he pulls his gun out and reloads. He blasts off six rounds. It helps clear out some space on the dock for me to swing my spear back and forth. I get some distance from the monsters. My spear chops off head after head. Devon drops the key into the ignition and cranks up the motor. The second it comes alive he hits the throttle. The boat pulls away from the dock. I feel fingertips brushing against my neck as I turn and take a running leap off the edge of the dock.

Chapter 12

There is no reason I should land this jump, but I do. Somehow I make it. My chest hits the side of the boat hard and my feet splash down into the water. I drop my spear into the boat and use both hands to get a grip on the railing. Behind me the infected push each other and fall into the water. As my grip starts to slip, Sara and Frank grab my arms and they pull me onto the boat. I am laid out next to Bob's body.

"Thanks Devon!" I cough up at him. He looks down over his shoulder at me.

"Sorry. I got excited."

The horrible island shrinks into the distance behind us. I feel a slight sense of relief. I did it. I helped this man. Frank pats me on the shoulder. We both have tears in our eyes.

"Where did you learn to shoot?" Sara asks him. Frank digs into a storage chest and pulls out a tarp.

"Boy Scouts," he grunts. I can't tell if he is feeding us a line or if he means it. I help him wrap up his brother.

"Thank you."

"Thank you for the ride," I stand up and look out across the bow. Vancouver is so close.

Frank sits in the passengers chair. He stares at the tarp. I have to get this guy to help me. With him and his gun by my side I could get home much faster. How do you ask a man that just lost his brother to help you find your family? How do you ask him to risk his life to help you save your loved ones?

"What's your plan?" I get a little closer. He shakes his head and shrugs his shoulders.

"I wanted to get my brother. After that, I didn't care."

"Do you have a place to go?"

"Bob had a cabin but I'd never been there. My place is...gone." I glance over at the controls. The gas gauge reads a quarter tank. So he is not getting too far in this thing, ten miles at best. We are close to the shore. Devon heads for a multi-million dollar home with a dock.

"I'm going home to my wife and kids."

"Lucky you," he raises his hand to put the revolver to his temple. Instinct takes over and as his hand comes up I hammer fist down onto his forearm. He pulls the trigger when we make contact and the round whizzes over my head, inches from my skull. I go deaf. I lose my equilibrium and fall backwards onto Devon. He is pushed forward and hits the throttle. The boat launches at the dock. Devon turns the steering wheel and pulls back on the gas but it is too late. We slam into the corner of the dock. The boat grinds along the edge and the hull tears open. The impact throws us all to the deck. We cruise right for the shore. Unable to stop, the boat slides up onto the rocky beach. The blades of the propeller chew up the rocks. I reach up and turn the key and the engine goes dead.

"Everyone okay?" I lay on my back testing for broken body parts. I'm fine.

"Yeah," the kids groan. I roll over to Frank and slide his gun away. I grab him by his collar and pull him close to my face.

"What the fuck are you doing?!" my jaw tightens. He shakes his head. "I know it's bad! I lost my best friend today! I don't know if my wife and kids are alive! You think you have nothing to live for?! Look around, man!" Frank looks at Sara and Devon. They are terrified.

"I need you. We need you!" I pull out my wallet and open it up and show Frank a picture of my family.

"Look at these girls. They could be your granddaughters," Frank sobs and grabs at me. He fights against me.

"They need me Frank...I need your help...we could be a team," I lay it on thick, but men are goal oriented. You give a man a project and they can excel. This is why men like to join the service and play football. Most men love to be part of a team that has a common goal. If I can get Frank on my team he might have a good reason to stick around.

"Please, sir. Stay with us," Sara utters. Frank looks over at her. His grip loosens. He looks back at the photo of my family.

"Okay. I'll stay."

"Are you solid?"

"Yeah. That wasn't like me...I don't..." he mutters. He is shaky, but if we can get him moving he might snap out of it.

"It's okay," Sara rubs her sore shoulder.

"What do you need off this boat?"

He points to a duffle bag in the corner of the boat. I pick it up and it is extremely heavy.

"What's in here?" I hand it to him.

"Ammo and more guns," he takes the bag, slings it over his shoulder and reloads his revolver.

The little beach we landed on is connected to a very well manicured yard. It is like a golf course. Amazing flowers and trees

142

are perfectly placed. The yard leads to a ridiculously expensive mansion. The backyard is completely fenced off and there are no infected in sight. I take a big swig of water and make my way to the back of the boat. Up and down the beach there is nothing going on, nobody trying to leave by boat. No panicked families running from swarms of the dead. Maybe it is not bad here. Maybe the police were able to get it under control. I turn back to Frank.

"What about your brother?" I look at the tarp.

"We can't take him," Sara joins me. Frank nods his head and thinks for a minute.

"He wanted to be cremated," the words fight to get out.

"Okay, we'll do that," I look around and find a tank of gas.

I pick it up, then climb over the edge of the boat and drop down to the beach. Devon tosses me my spear and he climbs over. Frank helps Sara over the rail and gently lets her down. He takes a last look around. There is nothing that he needs. He slides over the edge. I twist the cap off the gas tank and toss some fuel up into the back of the boat. I pull out my lighter.

"You wanna light it?" I offer my lighter. He shakes his head no. "You should back up," they step back and climb up onto the short grass. I light some of the fuel that splashed on the edge of the boat. It does not take long before the vessel is covered in flames. I catch up to the three of them on the lawn.

"He was a good little brother," the words fall out of his mouth. "I wasn't always the best brother…brothers fight and I wouldn't pull my punches…I told myself it made him stronger…he was always there for me…I will miss…I loved…" he turns away from the fire and makes the saddest whimper I have ever heard. Sara puts her arm around his shoulders. He drops his head and cries like a baby on her. The boat burns and burns. The wood snaps and pops. Chunks of the boat fall to the beach. My fear is that this is not the last time I will see a funeral like this. Sudden, no time to mourn, and ending in fire.

We stand there for a long time. I keep a look out, but I don't want to rush him. After a good amount of time he lets go of Sara and pats her.

"Thank you," he wipes his eyes over and over. The tears have stopped but he keeps drying them. I put my back to the river and take a good look at the house attached to this yard. It has a large back patio and is covered in beautiful stone. There is a big hot tub, built in barbecue, outdoor TV and furniture. A large sliding glass door gleams in the sunlight. I head for it.

I limp up to the eleven-foot tall door, cup my hands around my eyes and scan the room. Holy shit. There is a man in his eighties reading in a high back leather recliner. He puffs on a pipe. I gently knock at the window. He does not look up. I knock a little louder and this time he hears it. Up in the air goes his finger, "one moment please" and he picks up a bookmarker from the side table and slips it into his book. It takes a lot of effort but he stands up and puts the book back on the shelf behind him. He walks slowly over to the door and unlocks it, gives the door a hard pull and it slides open. He gives us a look.

"Can I help you?" his voice is raspy from years of smoking. He notices the gash on my forehead, broken nose and the way I favor my right leg.

"Son, what happened to you?"

"I've had a tough day."

He steps away from the door, "Come in. Lock the door behind you. The world has lost its mind. I am Calvin Ramsey, Attorney at law," he says it like he is doing a voiceover for a commercial.

I step into his home and it is as amazing as the outside. Devon is the last one through the door. He locks it and gives it a good pull to test it. The old guy shuffles away and down a hall. It is a three thousand square foot living room and kitchen. The ceiling is vaulted and you can see up to the second floor walkways. Everything here is top notch. On the walls and shelves he has a large collection of mounted dead animals from this region of the world.

"Where did he go?" Sara moves farther into the living room.

"I don't know."

"Maybe he went to get a gun," Devon grabs my arm. Maybe he did. Why the hell would he open his doors to this motley crew? On the wall hangs a portrait of our new host standing next to a beautiful woman. There is a noticeable age difference but she is definitely not his daughter. He shuffles back around the corner with a black bag and a little medical kit.

"One of you might be able to use this," he waves me over. "Come on boy it's heavy," I move quickly and help him. I take the bag. He points at the countertop island in his kitchen. "Put it there," I lay the bag up onto the granite. "After I retired I needed a hobby, so I took up taxidermy," he puts the medical kit on the island. "You folks look quite thirsty. Help yourself to whatever is in the refrigerator," the group is as confused as I am.

"How did you get all banged up?"

"Car crashes mostly. Took a bad fall. Punch to the face."

Calvin breathes in a light laugh at my answer and then looks over at the group.

"Go ahead and help yourselves." The others move into the kitchen and open up the big built in refrigerator door. It is full to the brim with all kinds of good food, cans of pop and bottles of beer.

"You want anything?" Devon pulls out a pop.

"Beer," without hesitation. Devon pulls out three bottles hands one to Frank, Sara and then me. It is a nice craft Indian Pale Ale and it goes down smooth.

"My old taxidermy kit is in the black bag. Whichever one of your friends has the strongest stomach can stitch you up. I would help but," he holds up his hands and they shake, badly. He shuffles out to the living room, picks up his book and sits back down on his recliner.

I look at the three people in the kitchen. Two are strangers and Devon is, well Devon. Frank sips at his beer and stares out the back window at the smoke cloud above his old boat. I am not going to ask him to stitch me up. So it is the two kids.

"All right. I'm bleeding a lot. I need you to stitch me up," they want no part of this, but I need these wounds cleaned up. I do not want to get home to my family and die from an infection. I put down my spear and take off my backpack. I down the rest of my delicious beer and climb up on to the island countertop.

"What are you doing?" Sara inquires.

"Yeah…we're not stitching you up."

"I can't do it myself. I'm not happy about it either, but I need these wounds stitched up." I can't believe I am asking them to drag a needle through my skin. When I was a kid I remember a nurse needed to draw some blood. I was not going to let them take it. I fought, cried and would not give my arm over to the lady. I must have embarrassed my poor Mom so much, but I knew that needle was going to hurt. My Mom pleaded with me to let them take the blood. She was supposed to be on my side. Why would she be on the bloodthirsty old nurse's side? Finally the nurse put the needle down and picked up the phone.

"I'm going to have to call your father at work," it was all she had to say. My arm was down on the table in a second. My poor Dad, he was not abusive or mean. We would get a spanking if we did something bad, but at the time that was a normal thing for parents to do. He was a good loving father and my parents are still together today. It all worked out in the end. They got their blood. Mom did not tell Dad I was acting whacky at the doctors and I learned you would not die from a little needle.

I stare at them until they give in. They wash their hands in the sink and then they find a set of rubber gloves in the medical kit.

"Calvin, do you have any hard booze?" I request. He looks up from his book.

"In the upper cabinet," he motions. Devon opens the cabinet and pulls down a bottle of vodka. I reach out for the bottle and take it from him. It is some top shelf booze. I have not had any top shelf cocktails since my kids were born. I twist off the top and take a swig. It is smooth, and makes my throat and stomach feel warm.

"You will want to clean the tools with this," I hand the bottle back to him. I feel the effects of the beer and vodka in my brain already. I have not eaten much today and the little bit I did eat was lost on the side of the road in Portland.

"I think this is a bad idea," Devon puts the bottle down on the countertop.

"Me too, but I don't have a lot of choices here do I?" I swallow hard. My throat still feels warm from the vodka. I don't normally drink straight booze like this. I am nervous and want to numb myself a little more so I take one last swig before they start.

"I have some painkillers if you want them, but they will knock you out for the rest of the day," Calvin asks.

I wish I could say yes and down the pills, but I do not have the time.

"No thank you. We need to get moving as soon as we're done."

"Suit yourself," he turns a page in his book.

Sara has found a kit from the black bag. It has needles, thread and some needle nose pliers.

"Have either of you ever stitched anything before?" I hope for a beneficial answer.

"No, not really," Sara looks to Devon.

"Yeah, but it's been a while," he gathers up a smile for me. I guess it was to make me feel better, but it didn't.

Calvin turns a page in his book, "After you clean the wound and thread the needle take the two pliers there in the kit and use them to start stitching at the top of the wound," he says not ever looking up from his book. What a weird old guy. He is going to sit there and read his book as a stranger preforms surgery on his kitchen counter.

"You heard the man," I lay back down onto the granite.

Sara gives into the fact that this has to be done and takes the lead, "Lets clean this out," she picks up the bottle of alcohol and a pack of gauze from the medical kit. She pours a little alcohol onto the pad.

I grab Devon by the wrist and pull him closer to me, "This is going to hurt. A lot and I'll need you to hold me still," I wait for him to nod at me so I know he understands.

"Okay, Okay," he looks over to Sara. She is ready with the gauze to clean my forehead. I fold my hands across my stomach and Devon puts all of his weight down on my arms.

"Sorry," she gives me a tense smile. Every muscle in my body is flexed.

"Let's get it over with," I give her a wink. She puts the gauze to my forehead and I scream out at the top of my lungs. I start sweating immediately. My body convulses. I fight to keep myself on the table. All I want to do is punch everyone in this room and we have not started on the stitches yet. This was a really bad idea. I can't keep my hands on my stomach anymore. I grab Devon.

"Dude, you're hurting me," he struggles to free himself from my grip.

"Don't call me dude!" I yell in his face. It feels like Sara is peeling my forehead off. My legs kick down onto the countertop.

"Stay still!" she commands. I focus on one of the animals on the wall. It is a squirrel, perched on a tree branch. It is amazing how life like it is. I think to myself *at least I am not the stuffed squirrel.*

I get into a zone and let go of Devon. She is done cleaning the cut and has the thread strung onto the needle.

"Now what?" she asks Calvin.

"Start at the top and make the stitches even. You want the skin to meet up and not overlap," he turns another page of his book. The guy is a fast reader. *At least I am not the stuffed squirrel.*

"Are you ready?"

"Yeah," the pain is so bad I can only speak monosyllabic. I look up at her and our eyes meet. The alcohol still burns in my forehead. Her eyes are dark brown and she is one of the prettiest girls I have ever seen this close up. Her hair is beyond red and her skin is alabaster white and lightly freckled. She looks like an Irish beauty queen.

I put out my hand and Devon takes it. We hold each other's grip like we are about to arm wrestle. Sara moves in close with the pliers in each hand and the needle is ready to go. I close my eyes. She pulls the needle through my skin.

"FFUUCCKK!" I call out. *At least I am not the stuffed squirrel.* I can feel her work quickly, but it is not fast enough. The needle pops in and out of my skin. Suddenly Frank is by my side. He stands next to Devon. My eyes open as soon as I feel his presence. I glance at Devon. Oh boy, the look on his face. I am squeezing his hand so hard that he looks like he is the one with a needle going in and out of him.

"Where are we going?" Frank asks. It is like he has no concept of what is going on. I can't answer him. I feel my eyes blink wildly, but my mouth will not open.

"Where do you live? Where is your family?" he asks again. He leans close. His eyes are blood shot. His breath smells of cheap coffee and expensive beer, "Think about it. Tell me where is your family."

My mind flashes to my family and my street address. I am not saying I don't feel the string pulling through the hole in my head, but suddenly it does not hurt as bad.

"We live off Mill Plain and 136th," the words burst out of my mouth. I see what he is doing.

"The kids, how old?"

"Valerie is five and Robin is two."

"That's a good age. Mill Plain and 136th? That's not too far, about four or five miles. You'll be home soon,"

"Done," Sara says. She snips the thread and goes to work wrapping a bandage around my skull.

"Thank you. Thank you. I need a few minutes before you start on my leg," I loosen my grip on Devon. She finishes taping up the bandage and I sit up. I feel the wrap around my head and it seems secure. I look over at our host. He turns another page in his book, "Have you heard anything about what's happening in Vancouver?"

"No, I have not," he readjusts his glasses.

"You know there is an infection?"

"Yes, but I do not have any current knowledge as to the state of our city," he looks up at me.

"Don't you wanna get out of here?" Devon asks.

"Where would I go? I am not able to protect myself from this plague. I would not dare inconvenience your party with my care. So I will stay put. This is my home. My wife died in this house and I will join her soon," he says quite matter-of-factly. He knows what he wants and has come to terms with it. I guess I can admire that. It is his time and he is not going to fight it.

"Okay, I'm ready," I pull up my pant leg and look at the damage done by the rock. My tattoo is ruined. I will not cry any tears over that, but the wound is jagged and longer than I thought it would be, "Shit!" I lay back down onto the countertop.

Sara gets a new bit of gauze and pours alcohol onto it.

"My hand can't take anymore. It really hurts," Devon keeps his distance.

"It's okay. I'm sorry if I hurt you," I give the kid a smile. Frank steps up and offers me his hand and I take it, "Go ahead." I tell Sara.

She puts the gauze to my leg and oh mama it hurts. I squeeze Frank's hand and he squeezes right back. This guy has one hell of a grip. She gets it cleaned and Devon hands her the threaded needle. Devon holds down my leg as Sara starts to stitch. I bite at my lips. *At least I am not the stuffed squirrel.*

"What's our plan?" Frank questions help keep my mind off my leg.

"We keep walking."

"It is five miles to your house. You want to walk all the way there?"

Tears stream out of my eyes and down the side of my face. The cut on my leg is so jagged that it is very difficult for her to sew up. *At least I am not the stuffed squirrel.*

"I do not believe you will be able to just walk out of here," Calvin rejoins the conversation.

"What do you mean?" Frank questions.

"I will show you when she is done," he turns another page.

"Almost there," Sara snips the thread and starts wrapping my leg.

Everything inch of my body hurts and I feel exhausted. I am drenched with sweat. Frank helps me sit up and pats me on the shoulder. Devon is right there with a fresh beer.

"Thank you," I sound like I am dead, but *at least I am not the stuffed squirrel.* I slide down off the countertop. I take a long drag off the bottle of beer.

"Show me what you're talking about." I limp away from the kitchen.

Calvin puts his book down and he fights to get up out of his chair. I follow him to the front of his house. He pulls back a curtain. I step up to the window to look. The front yard is beautiful of course. There is a private driveway and at the end of the driveway is a twelve-foot tall wrought iron fence. On the other side of the fence is a horde. A hundred infected monsters claw and press against the fence. My heart sinks. What am I going to do now? Is there a horde this size outside the front door to my apartment?

"We're fucked!" Is the only thing I can muster.

"Yes, you are." He pats me on the shoulder.

Chapter 13

The monsters push and pull at the iron fence. The metal groans under the weight.

"Why are they trying to get in here?" I whisper it to myself.

"That is my fault," Calvin refills his pipe.

"What?" I turn away from the window and face him.

"I saw one out there a few hours ago. The news said they are extremely deadly so I thought it would be a good idea if I took care of it. I got my old rifle and I shot at it from my bedroom window. Well, I missed," he again holds up his shaky hands, "I used all the ammo I had for the old rifle, but it only seemed to get their attention. After about twenty minutes of shooting there were thirty of them out there. Most of those poor souls are my neighbors. My apologies. I was not expecting company. I do not want any of you to worry. Even if they get through the fence the windows are safety glass. Every single window on the main floor could take a bullet and hold up." He lights up and puffs smoke everywhere.

"If they can push open that fence they can push open a window," Frank joins us in the foyer.

"How do we get out?" Sara steps up to the front window to get a better view. Calvin thinks about it as he takes a deep drag off his pipe. From outside there is a loud sound. I couldn't make it out at first so I step closer to the window next to Sara. The gate swings open. A chunk of brick has given way from the column that holds the locking mechanism. The sound we heard was five or six bricks falling to the concrete driveway.

"Damn it!" I throw my hands up and walk away from the door. Calvin reaches out and turns the bolt, locking it solid. The infected slowly push open the iron fence. The bottom of the gate grinds across the stone. They fall over each other and spill out onto the yard. In a minute they will have this place surrounded.

"What do we do?!" Sara backs away from the window. Devon reaches out and holds her shoulder.

"It's okay. Jim will think of something," they look over at me. I face them.

"I don't…" I stammer. The infected stomp up the porch. I turn away from the group and limp back into the living room.

"Hey!" Frank shouts after me. I head for the kitchen and they follow. Fists pound at the front door. I pick up my backpack and spear and I open up the back sliding glass door that we entered though. I stick my head out the door and there is already a group of them back here.

"Shit." I pull my head back in and slide the door shut. I barely get it closed when their bloody hands and faces slam up against the glass. I re-lock the door and turn back towards the group. It is too late, we are already surrounded. Calvin shuffles back into his kitchen and opens his fridge. He grabs the last Indian Pale Ale from the shelf, picks up the bottle opener and pops the cap.

"Where did you meet your wife?" Calvin takes a long swig.

"What? What are you talking about?"

"Your wife. Where did you meet her?"

"We don't have…"

"We have a few minutes," he cuts me off. I have to clear my head for a second and walk away from the monsters pounding at the window behind me.

"I was eighteen. It was my first day of college. To be a full time student you needed to take twelve credits. I had eleven and was looking for a one credit class. I found a one day a week karate class and signed up for it last minute. I got to the class and there she was, tall, thin and bright red hair. She wore jean cut off shorts. Shortest shorts legally allowed, full on Daisy Dukes. She had just moved from Arkansas and had a sweet little Southern accent. I was hooked," I look around the room at the group and they are all sporting smiles. It feels good to talk about something positive after the day I have had. My mind feels clear and able to think straight again. Calvin downs the last of his beer.

"What about you? How did you meet your wife?" I ask him. There is a very loud smash at the door. We hear the wood crack under the pressure.

"We do not have time for that," he takes the last puff of his pipe. The banging at the front door is louder and harder than before.

I limp to the front of the house and on the other side of the door is a giant bear of a human. Seven feet tall and four hundred pounds, crashing into the front door over and over again.

"Frank!" I call back into the living room. Frank already has his gun drawn. He aims at the monster as Calvin reenters the foyer.

"Wait!" Calvin cries.

"What's wrong?"

SMASH!

"Bullet proof glass. I told you every plate of glass on the main floor is bullet

proof. You shoot that and it will bounce right
back into this room."

SMASH!

"He's gonna bust down the door!" Sara
gets her machete up and ready for battle.

"Upstairs," Calvin is on the move and
heads back into the living room. He picks up
his book from the shelf and tucks it under his
arm.

We follow him down the hall away from the
living room.

SMASH!

Calvin steps into a doorway. It is an
elevator. An elevator in this house? Calvin
must have really done well for himself.

He puts his hand up and stops us from
entering.

"Weight limit, stairs around the corner,"
he hits the button and the doors close in our
faces.

SMASH!

We race down the rest of the hall and up
the flight of stairs. Calvin steps out of the
elevator as we crest the top of the stairs.

SMASH! THUD!

The door falls to the floor of the foyer
and they are in. At the top of the stairs is a
large bookshelf that holds Calvin's trophies
and treasures.

"Devon, help me!" I get on one side of
the cabinet and Devon gets on the other. We
push hard and the bookshelf tips, Calvin's
trophies slip and crash to the floor. It hits
the stairs and tumbles down to the first
landing, blocking the stairs. The infected are
in the living room. Blood falls off their
bodies and onto the hardwood floor. Black
colored ooze drips from their open veins and
splatters over the light carpet. They knock

over tables and chairs. Like their only goal is to destroy everything. What a shame. This house was beautiful. They see us at the top of the stairs. We follow Calvin down the second story walkway that overlooks the great room below.

Calvin opens a door and we file in behind him. It is the master bedroom. The room has high vaulted ceilings. There is also a couch and loveseat set and some large, heavy dressers in this room. Calvin locks the door behind us. Devon and I grab a dresser and slide it over to the bedroom doors. Sara and Frank grab the loveseat and push it next to the dresser. It will hold them for a while, but now what? We can't stay up here forever and there is no way to fight through them.

"How do we get out of here?" Devon whispers. I shrug my shoulders at him and look to Calvin. He gives me the same look. Frank is over by a window.

"Hey," he says faintly. I join him. The window is up high about four feet from the carpet. There is a lower section of roof under us. It is a ten foot drop down and at the far end of the roof are a couple of sun windows.

"Calvin, what's down there?"

"The garage," it hits him and he reaches into his front pocket. "Here, you can take my car," he hands the key to Sara.

"If we get down onto the roof I bet we can get in through the windows," Frank holsters his gun. I pop the lock and slide the window open. Frank and I work to get the screen out.

"Get some sheets tied up," I order Sara and Devon. Calvin shuffles over to the couch and turns on a reading light. He opens up his book to the bookmark. Sara and Devon find a closet and pull out a set of sheets. They work at tying the ends together. I open a closet to pull down two wooden dowels. This must have been Calvin's wife's closet. It is bursting full of lady clothes. I struggle to take two dowels full of clothes down. Once I get them free I grab a stack of sheets. I tie one of the sheets around the pieces of dowel.

"Make another set for the window into the garage," they move quickly and get to work on it.

"What about Calvin?" Sara pulls a knot tight.

"He can't climb out the window," Devon tosses the next set of sheets to the floor.

"What do you want us to do, Calvin?" I ask. He looks up from his book.

"I want you to find your family. I am good here. I only have four more chapters to go and I am done with this old book," he gives us a smile. The monsters are loudly tearing at the bookshelf on the stairs. They will be at the bedroom door soon.

"They will get in," Frank says in despair.

"I am not overly worried about it. Now go and be safe," Calvin pulls out his hearing aids and that is that. He can't hear us beg to save him. He can't hear the monsters banging down the door to kill him. It is just him and his book. I walk over and take a knee. I reach out to shake his hand. He grabs my hand, his shakes uncontrollably. I can't tell if that's how bad it normally is or if he is terrified.

"Thank you," I say loudly.

"You are welcome," he answers a little louder. I get back to my feet and help my crew prop up the dowel as an anchor in the windowsill. We toss the sheets out the window

and help Sara up. She has a good grip on the
sheet and slowly lowers herself. She lands on
the roof and stands one foot on either side of
the apex. The infected are milling about on
all sides of the garage. They have not noticed
us yet. She steadies herself, and then steps
away from the sheet. Devon and I tuck our
spears onto our packs. Frank and I help the
kid up into the window. They are at the
bedroom door. They got passed the bookshelf.
Sara is halfway to the sun windows. Devon has
hit the roof. We toss him the other dowel and
sheets. He catches it and turns to follow
after Sara. There is a large BOOM at the
bedroom door. Both Frank and I jump from the
sound. Calvin didn't notice. He must be very
deaf to not hear that one. Our big friend is
here and he hits the door with everything he
has.

I give Frank a boost up into the window.
He is off balance because of his heavy bag and
has a hard time getting a good grip on the
sheet. I hold his hand as he grips the window
frame. Frank gets his feet planted against the
side of the house. He is about to let go of
the window to grab the sheet when the big
monster punches through the door. My head
snaps around to see what happened. Calvin
jumps up from the couch. My grip on Frank's
hand slips. He slides out the window and down
the sheet. He lands hard on the roof and slips
to his butt. Calvin shuffles off to lock
himself in his bathroom. The big guy punches
another hole in the door. I look out the
window and Frank holds onto the peak of the
roof with one hand and his bag with the other.
He almost lost the bag of guns and ammo.

"DEVON!" I shout down to him. He turns
and sees that Frank is in trouble. The

infected notice that they are on the roof and they move toward the garage and claw at the siding. I grab a chair and stick it in front of the window and climb onto it. The big monster pushes the bedroom doors open. The dresser and love seat only slow him down. I get both legs up and out the window and look back at the monster. He is fully in the bedroom and trucks right for the window. I am not ready to let go of the solid wood frame and grab this flimsy sheet, but I can't wait anymore. It charges like a bull for the window. I let go of the frame and grab the sheet. I slide down quickly. The monster hits the window so hard he breaks the dowel and I fall to the roof. It is a five foot drop. I was not ready to free fall. The infected giant blasts out the window and shards of glass rain down on us. He is so big that he can't fit out the window. Only his head and shoulders stick out. I stare at it the whole time I fall. My feet hit the same sloped side of the roof and they slip out from under me and I land on my ass. It kills my ankle and I yell out in pain as I quickly twist and catch the peak of the roof with the tips of my fingers. I am on the other side of the peak from Frank. I pull myself up. Devon gets to Frank and grabs his wrist. I get the tip of the roof up under my armpits and reach out for Frank to pass me the heavy bag. I get ahold of the bag and Frank grabs Devon's other hand. We fight to get ourselves upright. I straddle the roof and hand the bag back to Frank.

"Do me a favor. Take care of that tub of guts," I point a thumb over my shoulder. Frank catches his breath and re-slings the bag. He pulls out his revolver and BOOM. He gets it right in the forehead. Bullseye. The monster slumps over and blocks up the window so none of the other infected creatures can get out that way. My ears ring from Frank's gun. As the ringing trickles off we hear a horrible sound coming from inside Calvin's bedroom. Screams. Worse than any I have heard today. I look at Frank and then Devon. Their faces have the same look of disgust that I feel deep in my heart. That poor old man, he did not deserve to die like that. He seemed like a good man and now...now he is being shredded by the hands of those disgusting monsters. I nod in the direction of the windows and we move.

We creep across roof and reach the windows. Sara sits perched at the top of the roof above the first one. The roof has a fairly steep pitch to it. If you move slowly it is not so bad but if you start to slide you will definitely fall over the edge. I prop myself up at the top of the first glass window. It is about two feet by four feet in size. It will be tight but we should all be able to fit. Devon locks his arm under my armpit and Frank does the same on my other side. They hold me tight. I slide down on my butt to get close to the window. I use the heel of my boot to kick down into the glass and my boot bounces off the glass. The next time I use both feet. I come down on the window hard. It shatters under the pressure. I slide over to the right of the window. Devon and Frank lower me down the roof so I am parallel with it now. I am able to let go of them and grab the edge of the frame.

"Pass me the dowel," I reach up as Devon lowers the piece of wood to me. I place it at the base of the window and drop the sheet down into the garage. The window sits about fifteen feet above the concrete floor.

"Slide down here next to me," I signal to Devon. Frank and Sara help him move slowly down to me. I help prop him up next to me. "Okay, Sara come down," Frank holds her hand and she slides down next to Devon.

"We're gonna lower you," she takes my hand and then Devon's. Sara drops her legs down into the window and slides her butt over to the edge. Together we lift her up and over the window and then slowly drop her down so that she is eye level with the dowel.

She lets go of Devon to grab the sheet. For a couple of seconds I am the only thing keeping this girl in the air. I freak out, just a little, but once she has ahold of the sheet I know she will be okay.

"Got it!" she breathes heavily. We let go of each other and she climbs down. When she gets to the end there is a couple feet drop but she lands it perfectly. It is dark down there.

"I'm fine!" she calls up at us. Seconds later she finds a light switch and kicks it on.

"Frank, come help me with Devon," Frank lets go of the peak and slides down. We set up the same as before and lower Devon down. It took every fiber of muscle to keep him from falling through the window when he let go of Frank. How I am going to get Frank down into this thing. Devon lands it with no problem.

"Toss the bag," I tell him. He lowers the bag down into the window and lets go. They catch it with a loud grunt. "You're gonna have to hold the dowel yourself," I tell Frank.

"It's no problem," he quickly drops his feet over the edge and wraps the sheet around his foot. He gets down onto the sheet all by himself. He gets to the bottom. Now it is my turn. I wrap my leg around the sheet like Frank did. I am sweating like a pig and my arms tremble. I use my foot to pin the sheet to my leg. My legs are holding most of my weight. I grab ahold of the dowel. It is not so much the physical act of dropping down into the window that is scary. It is the concrete below that scares me to death. If I fall I would break my ankles or snap my knees and then game over. Frank would have to put a bullet through my head. Why am I being so dramatic? Why am I concentrating on the bad? I need to stay positive. My family needs me to stay positive. This crew of people below needs me to stay positive. So, no more thoughts about falling and suffering a compound fracture, no more thoughts about becoming a cripple that slows the group down and gets everyone killed. No more thoughts about not seeing my family because I fell to my death. Oh my feet just touched down. That was not so bad. My muscles burn so I give my arms a good shake as I look around the garage.

Calvin drove a mid 2000's Toyota Camry. I feel weird. I guess I feel let down. The house was so nice I thought it would be something more exotic.

"What a bummer," Devon shakes his head with disappointment.

"Hey!" I whack him in the arm.

"What?" he rubs his sore bicep.

"Show a little respect. It has four wheels, what else do you need?" Sara whacks his other arm.

"Stop hitting me," he rubs his other arm.

The monsters claw at the garage door.

"Now what?" Frank and I look around the garage. It is so clean. Everything has its perfect place.

"We need something to clear a path to the street," I whisper. "Why don't we drive through them?" Frank asks.

"It will kill the car. This Toyota can't take many hits before we blow the radiator," Sara says leaning up against the drivers' door. I open cabinets and look through shelves. I don't know what I am looking for. Something to distract them would be nice, but it is a normal garage filled with tools, cleaning rags and Christmas decorations. I open the last set of cabinets and I find what I was looking for. I pull out two propane tanks. They must be extras for his outdoor barbecue.

"Sara, pop the trunk to the car," I grunt as I carry the two heavy tanks. She pulls out the keys from her pocket and opens the trunk. Calvin seemed like the type to always be prepared. I was right, there in his trunk is an emergency kit. I drop the tanks and open the kit. It has exactly what I am looking for. Road flares.

"What are you thinking, bro?" Devon scratches at his neck.

"We're gonna Duct Tape these flares to the tank. Pop the flare and roll them out under the garage door. Frank shoots them. Boom. What do you think?"

"That's idiotic." Sara shuts the trunk.

"You want to open the door?" Devon shakes his head and thumbs at the garage door.

"What if it blows the door down on us?" Sara shakes her head at me too.

"It's all I got," I rest my hands on my hips. They look at each other and shrug their shoulders.

"Lets do it," Frank nods his head. I grab the roll of Duct Tape off the work bench. I also pull a drawer out of the tool box. It is full of all different sized screwdrivers. I tape a flare to the side of the tank and then I tape down over twenty screwdrivers to each tank. I hope when it blows it will fire these screwdrivers in all directions, taking down a few more of them. Devon and I drag the tanks over next to the car. Sara and Frank push the big toolbox. It is a heavy-duty steel box that is thirty-six inches wide, and they push it over to the garage door. If we stay behind it we will hopefully be safe from the explosion. Frank picks up a drill out of the toolbox and puts a one-inch bit on it. He drills a hole into the garage door. I unhook the garage door so that the chain is not pulling it open or closed anymore. Now I can lift it open myself and close it when we are done. I grab a wrench and stick it into the track that holds the wheels. I set it so that we can lift the door about two feet before the wrench stops the door from going up any higher.

I look through Frank's newly drilled hole and there are nearly forty of them milling around out there. I need to get the tanks as far away from the door as I can, but there are so many infected in the way. If one of them steps in front of it and blocks the tank we will be in trouble.

"Devon, you open the door. I'll roll out the tanks. Sara you be ready to cut down anything that climbs under the door. Frank, clear me a path," I give Devon a nod and he pulls up on the door. It stops against the wrench and the foul smell of them rushes into the garage. Frank fires six rounds.

"Now!" He yells. I pop the top off the flare. It fires up and burns hot next to my hand. I take a run at the door and then release the first tank like a bowling ball. I give it everything I got. I let out one hell of a grunt when the tank leaves my hand. I angle it to the right. Devon drops the door right away. The tank rolls and rolls. Frank watches through the hole.

"We're good," Frank gives me a nod.

I grab the second tank. Devon lifts up the door. A set of busted up arms reach under the door and grab Devon by the shins. He squeals and let go of the door. It crashes down on the arms. Another set of fingers reaches under the door. They lift up the door and it comes to a stop at the wrench. Devon takes a few steps back. Frank steps on the handle of the garage door and stomps it down. The arms keep it from closing. Sara shoves Devon back as she strikes with her machete. She chops off the monster's arm. Then she rears back and takes another chop. The severed limbs gush black blood into the garage. Frank quickly fires six shots and pulls back up the garage door.

"Now!" he yells. I pop the flare and run for the door and sling this tank to the left. I grab the door and slam it shut with Frank.

"Look," Devon points down at his feet. I look back and the two arms are still attached to his shins. He does a little dance to shake them off. It takes a good bit of foot work to loosen their grip.

"Are we ready?" Frank has his gun up and ready to fire.

"Here," Sara hands me the car keys. I open the driver side door and put both Devon's and my spear into the car. We leave all four doors open so we are ready to roll. We group behind the toolbox and Frank takes careful aim. I plug my ears. Frank pulls back on the hammer and then squeezes the trigger.

BOOM and then BOOM!!! The garage door rocks and almost comes down off the tracks.

"Oh, God!" Frank's the only one that can see what has happened out there. He has already got the next tank in his sights.

BOOM! BOOM!!!

That one finished the job and the garage door falls fully off the tracks. Frank and Devon push the toolbox back out of the way. I give the door a good hard kick and it falls out and onto the driveway. The tanks put two massive craters outside the garage. Every one of the infected monsters are down on the ground. The ones closest to the blast were set ablaze. The screwdrivers and tank shrapnel absolutely shredded them. The monsters are laid out on the ground twitching and convulsing. It looks like a war zone.

"Jim!" Sara yells at me. I turn and the three of them are already in the car. Frank is in the passenger side and the kids are in the back. I pull the keys out of my pocket and run for the car. I start up the Toyota. I drop it down into low and hit the gas. We ride quickly out of the garage and over the fallen door. It is hard to describe the sound of our tires as they crush the skulls of the infected. It is kind of a pop, but with a lot of crunch, a squish and squirt. We roll over twenty of them to get to the gate. I pull the car up to the end of the driveway. I look at myself in the rear view mirror.

I look ridiculous with this bandage on my head. Why am I the one driving? I am sure I have a concussion. I have black eyes now from my broken nose. I look back at the house. The infected flood the front yard. I turn the steering wheel to the right. This is a little road that connects all these million dollar homes on the riverfront. The road is clear. No cars blocking the way, no infected roaming around looking for their next meal. I step hard on the gas and then the car dies. We come to a complete stop. I look down at the console. The gas gage reads empty.

"No!" I hit the steering wheel. What the hell! I turn the key again and nothing. The starter tries to turn the engine over but it does not catch.

"What happened?" Sara yells.

"We're out of gas!" Frank groans. I turn the key again and pump the gas and keep one eye on the rearview mirror. I watch the horde get closer and closer.

Chapter 14

When I was in college I had an old Volkswagen Rabbit. It had chronic electrical problems. Actually it had a leaking problem. Every time it rained, water would leak somewhere in the windshield-dash area and drip down onto the electrical circuits. Sometimes the lights did not work. Sometimes the blinkers did not work. Most of the time it would not start and I would have to reach up under the dash, give the electrical box a wiggle and then it would come back to life. I got used to having an unreliable car. Worse case scenario involved calling a tow truck. It was a pain in the ass and it cost me money, but I loved the car. It was the first one I had bought with my own money so it had a special place in my heart. It was also the car I first made out with my then girlfriend and now wife, so it had real sentimental value. Never in the three years that I owned it, was my life in danger if it did not start. As the four of us sat here in Calvin's car an extreme sense of dread fills my core.

I try again and again to start the thing, but it will not turn over. The infected have surrounded us. They scratch at the windows and bang on the roof. My three passengers scream at the top of their lungs for me to do something. As a father you develop a level of tolerance to all kinds of noise. You can tune it out to a certain degree. The amount of noise, panic and despair I am going through would cripple the average father. I look out my window and face a creature so horribly disfigured, the fact that it is still up and walking around is a crime against nature. There is more bone showing than anything from the neck up. Milky eyes floating in a red skull is a good way to describe it. The jaw is held on by only the slightest of muscle fibers. The tips of its fingers have been worn away and now only the bones remain. Over the screams I hear the tapping of its hand on my windowpane. I turn the key again and the engine starts. I can't believe it. I waste no time and punch the gas.

We tear out of the driveway and leave the disgusting freaks behind. I get the Toyota up to sixty and we all let out a triumphant yell. In the rearview mirror I watch as they follow us out onto the street.

Every house we pass looks as nice as Calvin's. A nice little community of million dollar homes right on the riverfront. We are almost to the intersection we need to turn onto. After the turn it is all uphill for a few miles. If this car is anything like my Mitsubishi the second we start up the hill the gas moves around in the tank and it will cut off again.

Frank pulls his bag up into his lap. He unzips it, pulls out a black case and digs around a little more and finds a shoulder harness. It is a double gun harness, one under each armpit. He opens the case and there is a set of matching nine millimeter Berettas. Frank pulls out four clips and he slides one into the bottom of each gun. He puts one gun into each holster, drops the leather straps down onto his shoulders and clips it to his belt. In a few seconds it is strapped to his body and ready to go. The last two clips slide right into his front pants pocket. He digs a little more into his bag and pulls out a small revolver. It is already in a holster and he wraps it around his right ankle. By my count the man has about thirty to thirty five shots before he has to reload. From the bottom of the bag he pulls out a big black gun.

"What's that?"

"SKS."

It looks like an AK-47. It fit in his bag because the stock has been sawed off and it looks like its barrel is shorter than normal. He snaps the banana clip into the bottom of it. Then he pulls out a second clip and a roll of electrical tape. Frank quickly tapes the two clips together.

"Holy moly!" Devon sounds like a kid at Christmas.

"What?" grunts Frank.

"Can we have some guns?" Devon begs. Frank turns back and looks at him.

"You know how to shoot?" Franks says flatly.

"No," Devon's eyes drop.

"I don't want to get shot by a kid."

I hang a left. It is a slight hill at first, but the Toyota keeps moving. It feels good to be on a road that is not heavily traveled. There are no cars and trucks whizzing by at a hundred miles an hour. No big rigs or snow plows destroying every vehicle on the road. We cross over the train track. There are a few abandoned cars I have to swerve around. The next road we are going to cross is a major highway that runs from downtown Vancouver almost all the way to Idaho. We round the last bend in the road and there is the highway. Traffic is moving. I can't believe it. There is no crowd of dead people smashing from car to car eating the passengers.

"There's a gas station right there," I point up on the hill on the other side of the highway. At the intersection a nice soccer mom waves me through and we take off up the hill.

"That was weird," Devon looks out the back window at the cars patiently waiting their turn. On and off the highway they go like nothing has happened today. There is no one at the next intersection so I blow through the red light and turn into the gas station. The Camry runs rough as we pull up to the pump. We survey the area.

"Looks clear," Frank pops open his door.

"How much should I get?" I pull my wallet out and get my debit card ready.

"Fill it if you can," Frank grunts as he steps out of the car.

Sara looks over at the convenience store part of the station. "We should get supplies. Water and some food."

"I'll like go with her," Devon volunteers. I pop the door open and step out. My neck kills but I keep my head on a swivel. Devon and Sara climb out and head for the front door of the store. Frank stands guard by the passenger door. I slide the card into the machine and grab the nozzle. I watch Sara and Devon fill a basket in the store. The pump fires up and drops gas into the tank.

A big truck pulls into the station. A rough redneck type is at the wheel. He screeches to a stop and rolls down his window.

"They still got beer?" he calls down to us.

"I think so."

"Cool. Shit's gettin' fucked up man," he pops his door and steps down.

"Yeah, shit is gettin' fucked up."

"I'm gonna get me some supplies and head up to the mountains. Let this shit settle for a few days," he walks by me for the front door. He catches a glance at Frank and puts his hands playfully up in the air.

"Relax partner. I mean you no harm," he laughs to himself as he steps into the store. Frank and I look at each other. He is as confused as I am. People handle crisis differently. I remember the famous photo taken during hurricane Katrina of a man toting a bucket full of beer as he struggles through waist high water. Priorities man. The gas pump stops and it is full. I put the nozzle back.

"COME ON GUYS!" I shout at the kids. I look back into the store and see a man holding a gun on them and the redneck.

"Damn it!" I take off for the front door. Frank is right behind me.

"You have to pay for that!" yells the clerk. I step into the store and he points the gun at me. I stop in my tracks and put my hands in the air. The clerk takes a look at Frank.

"Oh, shit!" the clerk and Frank have each other in their sights. The man's gun shakes as he whips it from Frank back over to the redneck. The redneck has two cases of beer stacked in his hands.

"I can pay, man. Calm down," says the redneck.

"So can we," Sara points at me. "He's got money."

"Okay! I don't give a shit what the news says! I'm not getting looted!" the clerk steps back and gets behind the front desk. Sara walks over with her basket and sets it on the counter. The clerk puts his gun down and begins to ring her up. The second he looks down to scan an item the redneck bolts. The bottles of beer clank around in their boxes as he hits the door.

"Stop you son of a bitch!" the clerk yells after him. He snatches up his gun and runs around the counter. He kicks the door and it swings out wide.

BOOM, BOOM, BOOM! He guns the redneck down in the parking lot. He falls to his face and the cases of beer shatters on impact. We flinch and duck down behind the displays of magazines. The clerk leaves the store to check out his handy work and continues to scream at the man for stealing his beer. The redneck's body bleeds out on the asphalt.

"What should we do?" Sara and Devon have ducked down behind me.

"Stay down and be quiet," I pull out a knife from my belt. "Frank, what do you think?"

"I don't know. The guy shouldn't have nicked the beer," Frank keeps his SKS trained on the clerk.

The redneck slowly lifts himself off the forty-eight busted beers bottles. Blood pours out from his stomach. His eyes are black. The redneck has turned. The clerk fires off his remaining shots. He hits the infected in the chest. The clerk backs up quickly and trips on the curb. He falls hard to his back. The infected snaps his teeth and is about to pounce when its head explodes. The clerk looks back at the store and there is Frank, gun still smoking in his hand.

"Shoot'em in the head," Frank holsters his revolver.

"Thank you. Take what you have in the basket," he gets to his feet. "I owe you guys one."

Sara grabs up the basket of snacks and water.

"Lock the door. It's only gonna get worse," Frank picks up a couple packs of bubble gum. We race back to our car and pile back into the Toyota.

I take a long drag of water from my pack as I pull out of the gas station. I crank the wheel to the right and take off.

Vancouver is all suburbs. Thousands of homes wrapped around shopping centers. As we speed down the road we see families scramble. Clamber to fill their cars and SUV's with laptops, iPads and phone chargers. The housing development to our right is so packed on top of each other. The houses sit less than fifteen feet apart with no backyards. There is a five foot stone wall that separates their tiny backyards from the sidewalk. They are squeezed into tight streets and around culs-de-sac and in the center of it all there is a golf course. I hope everyone grabs their golf clubs before they leave. They are going to need more than iPads to fight against the infected. Sara and Devon load the new food and water into his backpack. They hand the over flow up to Frank to put into his bag.

"We're getting close," I tell them.

"What are we gonna do after we find your family?" Sara chomps down on an energy bar.

"I hope we can ride out this shit in the apartment, but I don't know."

"We should try and get to a Costco," Devon digs into a bag of jerky.

"That's a good idea," Frank re-zips his bag. "Tons of supplies and no windows. A big metal door that can be locked."

I weave the car past some newly infected humans.

The road we are zipping down runs parallel with a big highway. It is gridlocked in both directions. In the distance is a swarm of infected people. They are marching down the highway smashing windows and biting the terrified people. A couple of people stuck in this mess try and make an escape. They drive up onto the median and into the emergency lane. Whole families are consumed right in front of us.

I step on the gas and get the car up to seventy miles an hour. Calvin's ride has a smoother feel to it than my car. It really hugs the road at this speed. The closer we get to the freeway the more infected there are on the streets. I weave in and out of the traffic. Both my side mirrors are torn off by near misses with small groups of infected. The bloodthirsty monsters race off the highway and are storming towards us. They are a plague of locusts that devour crops of healthy humans.

"We have to get away from the highway!" Sara pulls herself forward with the back of my seat, her face right next to mine. I don't have much of a choice. The intersection up ahead has a multiple car crash blocking the road. It looks like some of the cars tried to escape the highway and crossed the little stretch of land that separated the two roads. They lost control and crashed into each other. The street and sidewalk are totally blocked. I am going to have to turn right and head north.

A car screeches to a stop on the other side of the intersection. He tries to smash his way through, but he only destroys his car. He stumbles out of his car. His shirt is covered in blood. There is a family in the front and back seats. He has a look of devastation on his face. He scans the chaos around him and then looks back at his car. The woman in the passenger's seat points at him and slams her fist down onto the dash. The children in the back seat slap their little hands at the glass windows. The horde on the highway closes in on him and his family. I make the turn. He pulls a gun from his belt and quickly fires three shots into his car. All four of us flinch with each shot. Little clouds of pink spray up onto the windows. The last thing the man does is put his pistol to his temple and pull the trigger.

"That motherfucker!" my face goes flush with anger.

The horrible scene shrinks in my rearview mirror.

"Would you want your family to turn?" Frank pulls out a stick of gum and pops it into his mouth.

"No!" I yell at him. With every minute that passes in Vancouver I feel more and more agitated. Seeing how bad it is this close to my home fills me with dread. Even in Calvin's mansion they were able to get in. Thinking about it makes my eyes water up. I notice my grip on the steering wheel. My hands are trying to tear the wheel off the column.

"We should try and find a farm to live on," Devon says as he pops the last of the jerky in his mouth.

"A farm?" I say over my shoulder at him. The thought of living on a farm has always been a little fantasy of mine. I know that the reality of owning and operating a farm is ridiculously hard work, but maybe with a group of people all helping out it could be possible.

"A farm," I say again to myself. I know outside of Vancouver there are tons of working farms. If we could get there maybe the owner would let us stay if we helped out. The more I think about it the better I feel. "That's a really good idea."

"You know how to farm?" Frank chews his gum loudly.

"No, but I could learn."

"I lived on one as a kid," says Sara.

"Really?" asks Devon.

"For like a year, but I didn't help or do any of the work. I was only six at the time," she finishes off the last of her energy bar.

"We could find a book that would tell us what to do," says Devon.

The little street we are on is lined by beautiful homes with big front yards. There are not too many people packing up and leaving these houses.

We are so close. It is only a mile until my apartment. I can already feel my family's arms around me. I can't wait to talk to Karen, and tell her about everything I have been through today. I know that she will love the idea of living on a farm.

"What's that?" Frank points out the windshield. I snap out of my daydream. There is a roadblock up ahead. Men and women stand behind barricades armed with assault rifles. There is about twenty of them out there and they are dressed in normal street clothes. On the ground and street outside of the barricades lay piles of dead bodies. I hope they are only gunning down infected.

"They don't look like police," Frank gets his gun ready.

"Or military," says Sara. As we approach they aim their guns at us.

"We should drive through them?" Devon ducks back behind Frank's seat.

"They'd cut us down in a heartbeat," Frank grumbles. All of the intersections we pass are labeled "Dead End." There is no way around them and I am absolutely not going back to the highway.

"Who are they?" Devon hands Sara her machete from the floorboard.

"I don't think it's going to help," she takes it anyway. They are set up outside the parking lot of a church. I stop the car. I stare them down and rev the engine a few times. A woman steps up to the side of the car. I totally didn't see her. Blindsided like how the raptors take down their prey in *Jurassic Park*. Clever girl.

"Don't try it buddy," she says to me. She taps the drivers side window with the tip of her gun. "Pull in," she waves us into the lot. I am out of moves. There is no choice. I pull into the parking lot. There are more people with guns at the front of the church. Another twenty or so with rifles strapped to their backs.

"Keep moving!" A man yells at us and he points to a driveway beside the church. At the front of the church there is a school bus unloading kids. The adults quickly move them through the double doors and into the building.

"How did they get so organized, so fast?" I ask. We loop around the back. There is another group of people waiting, also armed with guns. They have ten cars parked back here. The cars are set up so that they form a half circle around the back of the building. They are using the cars as another form of blockade.

"Get out!" a big man yells at us. He looks super pissed off and spits every time he talks. "I said get out of the fucking car!" he has a toothpick tucked into the corner of his mouth.

"We're so screwed! The're gonna kill us!" Devon opens his door. I turn off the engine and slowly climb out. We leave our spears behind. They take Frank's guns and his bag the second he opens his door. They grab my machete and knives I have strapped to my hip. They do the same to Sara and Devon.

"What do you want?" I ask.

"Shut up and get inside," the big man commands. He wears camo pants and a matching t-shirt. He is over six three and all shoulders and arms.

"Who are you people?" Frank glares at the big guy. He grabs Frank by the arm and forces him up to the back door of the church.

"Follow them," says a smaller guy also dressed in camo. He has Frank's bag slung over his shoulder. I follow Frank inside. Sara holds onto the back of my jacket as we enter the doorway. It reminds me, I do the same thing to my wife every time we go to a haunted house. I make her lead and I hold onto her clothes. I really hate haunted houses and I do not care if it makes me look unmanly.

The place is a hive of people working. They carry up boxes from a set of stairs that lead to the basement below. They fill newly constructed metal shelves with canned food and medicine. There are even more guns lining the walls of the room. They have medical cots set up with people that look like doctors and nurses running the show. The man with Frank's bag walks us down a hallway. Another person follows the four of us and he has our blades. We are led to a door at the end of the hall. He opens it and turns on the light. It is a small room full of cleaning supplies, toilet paper and towels.

"Give us your drivers license," the man holds out his hand.

"What?"

"License, now," he snorts.

"Why are you doing this?" Sara voice cracks. The man reaches for the gun strapped to his leg. I pull out my wallet and he takes it from my hand.

"I'm trying to get to my family," I grit my teeth.

"Okay," says the man.

"Please! Let us go! I have to get to them. I only live a mile away," he shoves me into the storage room.

"It is not up to me," he takes the rest of the wallets.

"Who's in charge?" Frank demands.

"Not you,"

"How long are you going to keep us?" Devon whimpers.

"That is up to Brother Paul."

"Who?" I stand right in the doorway.

"He is the man that will decide your fate," he slams the door shut in my face.

Chapter 15

The fluorescent light in the storage room buzzes above us. It casts an eerie glow, making us all look sickly and pale. There is no telling how long we are going to be in here. After a few minutes it hits me. We stink. All the blood, sweat and tears have made us a stinky bunch of people. I sweat a lot. Always have. In the summer, at work, I would have to take paper towels and fold them in half then jam them up into my armpits. I call them my "no-sweats" and they would soak up most of the overflow. They would keep my dress shirts from pitting out. Nobody wants to buy a laundry set from a guy with sweat stains from his ribs to his elbows. It only happens on warm days and under my right arm pit mostly. Days like today would give me the double stains and right now these puppies are working overtime. They are cooking up a super stink and my three partners in crime are suffering the worst of it. I pace back and forth which does not help with the sweat factory I have going inside my shirt.

Devon is propped up against a wall. He has not moved or looked up at us since we were jammed in here. Sara nervously chomps on her fingernails. Every now and then she will get a chunk torn off and spit it to the floor. From out side we hear shouts and commands. Then someone will run up and down the hall. Frank has found a cozy spot on the floor and he sits with his legs crossed in a meditation pose. Out of the inside pocket of his jacket, he fishes out a pack of smokes and a lighter.

"There has to be a way out," Sara spits another chunk to the floor.

"We're outmanned and outgunned. They've got us for as long as they want us," Frank slips a cigarette between his lips.

"Why would they like want our licenses?" Devon keeps his eyes focused on the floor.

"I don't know," I throw a hard kick at the door out of frustration. It is a thick chunk of wood and well locked. It does nothing but make Sara jump.

"Sorry," I tell her. Frank fires up his smoke. He blows out an enormous cloud. Normally I would hate someone smoking close to me. Cancer and everything, but what does it matter now. The smoke smells better than we do.

"You think they're going to torture us?" Devon whispers.

"Why would you say that? They're church people!" Sara spits a bit of nail at him.

"People in churches do stupid shit all the time," Devon kicks it right back at her, "I saw this movie once. It was filmed in the seventies in Brazil. This church in a small town would give wine and women to the tourists as they passed through. Once they got them to relax and let down their guard. The church people would cook and eat them. It was so scary." There is a burst of gunfire. We all shutter.

"Damn it, that story isn't helping," I resume pacing.

The gunfire came from the front of the church. Maybe it is the infected. Maybe it is a car that would not stop.

"We should try and escape," Devon aims it at me.

"How?!" I stop pacing and face him.

"I don't know. You can think of something. You're always thinking up how to get out of things," he folds his arms in a pout. They didn't get Frank's ankle gun and I have my hammer in my backpack. I think Devon has an extra knife in his. A six shot revolver, a hammer and a knife versus an army of assault rifles. Great. At best we would take down the people that open the door. Then we would be murderers. I am not a murderer. I don't want to kill anyone. I didn't want to kill the guy in the Big 5. He pulled the trigger not me. My conscience is clear with that guy. I don't want an innocent person's blood on my hands. I have enough infected blood on them. I feel bad every time I kill an infected.

Here's my plan. We storm out of here stab, hammer and shoot the first couple of people. Then what? We would not make it fifteen feet from the door. They would slaughter us. We would be cut down in a hail of gunfire. Shot up in the backyard of a church. Why do I have to think of something? It is someone else's turn to come up with a plan to escape death. My phone vibrates. I pull it out quickly. I am so excited I almost drop it. It is my brother.

"Don?!" I yell.

"Jim? Can you hear me?"

"I can hear you," there is a long pause. "Don?" I ask.

"It shows that you're there but I can't hear you. We're safe. Get to Mom and Dad's. I love you bro. Get to Mom and Dad's. See you there," then he is gone. My folks live outside of Vancouver on five acres. It is not a farm. There are only grass fields around it. The house is large and surrounded by trees. It is a good place to fall back on. It is not easy to find if you haven't been there before. I hang up the phone and dial my wife. It rings and rings. It goes to her voicemail.

"Karen! I hope you can hear me! I love you and the girls! Please be safe! I'm almost home! I love you baby!" I hang up my phone and slide it back into my pocket. Tears spill down my cheeks.

"What are your kids' names again?" Frank is halfway done with his cigarette.

"Valerie and Robin," I choke a little on the words.

"How old?"

"Valerie's five. She just started school and loves it. Robin is two. She's a fiery redhead. Her hair looks a lot like yours." I point at Sara. When I think about my kids even a little my heart wants to explode. My wife can take care of herself. She can run and kill an infected if she has to. Kids do not understand. They will only be scared. "What about you? Any kids?"

"I had a boy," Frank leaves it at that.

Someone is at the door. Before it opens the lights go out and it is pitch black. I fucking hate the dark. Even as an adult I have a night light in my bedroom. It is not for the kids or my wife. It is for me. A second later the door opens and they blind us with a powerful light. I can't see anything.

"Turn around and put your hands in the fucking air!" they command. Hands push us to turn our backs to them. A black fabric sack is jammed down over my head. The asshole hits the gash on my forehead and the pain cripples me. My hands are pulled behind my back and zip tied. They drag me out of the storage room.

"What do you want?!" I shout.

"Let us go! Fuckers!" yells Sara.

The bag on my head is tightly woven. I can't see shit. They shove me down the hallway. I can't breathe. I have never been this afraid. None of the infected has filled me with this much outright terror.

I am forced to my knees. This is it. They are going to execute me. I am never going to see my family again. I will never see another sunrise. My family won't even know what has happened to me. I will end up in a shallow grave with a bullet to the skull. Maybe they will chop my head off and I will still turn. Then I will be a severed head, still chomping my rotted teeth and sitting next to my lifeless body in that grave forever. Fuck, I know how to depress myself.

Someone in the room works quickly at a computer keyboard. They type wildly and pause every now and then. A printer spits out sheet after sheet. Someone organizes a handful of papers at a desk in front of us.

"Jim Blackmore?" A powerful voice asks from behind the desk.

"Yeah!"

"Sara Foster?" the voice questions.

"Yes," she whimpers.

"Frank Ellwood?"

"Fuck you!" Frank declares. Now that is how you sound tough. Frank is going to get us killed, but he sounds grizzled.

"And Devon McKay?" poor Devon lets out a cry and a snort.

"Where are you all going?" asks the voice.

"Who wants to know?" Frank spits the words from his mouth.

"I am Brother Paul. I decide who stays and who goes. Now where are you going?" we don't answer. It's a trick. Devon yelps. They are torturing him. He screams like someone has pulled a fingernail out.

"My apartment!"

Devon lets out a soft cry. They have stopped hurting him.

"To find your family?"

"Yes!"

"Karen, Valerie and Robin?"

"How did you...?"

"I have your license and a working internet. I know everything. Now answer the question!"

"Yes! I'm trying to get back to my family!"

"Good. Sara, where are you going?"

"I'm with Jim, helping him find his family!"

"What. about your mother and father? Kristen and Ray?"

"They're dead!"

"How did they die? I do not see a record of that. Was it today?" Brother Paul shuffles some papers.

"Yes. They were bitten," she hyperventilates.

"I am sorry for your loss. What were you arrested for a few years back?"

"Spray painting a wall."

"Not just any wall, but the front of a church and your father worked there as a preacher. Why are you following Jim?"

"He saved me!"

"Did he? From what?"

"I was almost raped...and he saved me."

"Jim, you are a hero. Now Devon, where are you going?"

"With…Jim."

"And your parents? Travis and Susan? I see they live in West Linn."

Devon fights to form the words. "I don't know what's happened to them…I was at work."

"You work with Jim I see. Why did you stay? Why didn't you go find them?"

"I would have died. Jim saved me."

"He saved you too? Jim, you are a savior. Do you feel saved right now?" Devon cries.

"Frank-"

Frank cuts him off. "Dead son. Wife and brother eaten by freaks. Never arrested. Not even a Goddamn parking ticket. Let's get this shit over with."

"So hostile Mr. Ellwood? Did Jim save you too? Is there a theme here?" Frank doesn't say a word. "Please do not take The Lord's name in vain. Not in his house and not ever."

"Fuck you!"

"I am asking you politely not to swear. Well, I will get right to it. One last question. Are you good Christians?" It must be a trick. Why would he care? What does it matter if we are good Christians? The world is falling apart and he wants to tell us about Jesus. What are we supposed to say? I celebrate Christmas but don't go to church. Do I dare tell him the truth or what he wants to hear?

"It is not a trick question," Brother Paul walks over to us. I can feel his presence. He is only feet from us. A drink is poured. I can smell the alcohol.

"The world is coming to an end. My flock and I have been preparing for this Day of Judgment. We have spent years readying ourselves for the worst. It is only a matter of time before we are ushered into the loving embrace of our Lord, but until that day I must keep my people alive."

He is a good preacher. I will give him that. It is like listening to an incredible salesman. Every word is perfectly timed and given the exact inflection needed for maximum impact. Something trickles down my face and neck. It is difficult to tell if it is blood or sweat. My forehead throbs with pain.

"What I really want to know is, are you evildoers? It sounds silly, I know. Evildoers. What I mean is, there will be no law enforcement after today. No one to police the masses. No one to watch if you have committed a crime. Against man or God. I do not want people running around Vancouver murdering every person they meet."

A gun cocks behind us. Devon and Sara let out soft whimpers. I am going to blow this bag off my head I am breathing so hard.

"I need to see my family again! Please! They need me!"

"I have no doubt that you would do whatever it takes to protect them, but I will also do whatever it takes to keep us safe." He moves around the room and sips his booze. "I am a busy man. So tell me, can I trust you to be good Christians?"

"YES!" I shoot the word from my mouth.

"And the rest of you?"

"YES!" They yell.

"I will only give you this one warning. If you cross me, I will make you and your families suffer." He moves back in front of us. He is face to face with me.

"Jim, I know everything about you. I know where all of your family members live. I trust you. I trust you to always do right. Know that I will hold you personally responsible for your people," he rests his hands on my shoulders. "God has told me that you are good.

He has whispered in my heart and revealed to me your true colors. I know you are a good man. A good family man, just like me," Brother Paul rubs my shoulders and gives them a little pat. His hands linger on my body. "Return their weapons and guns. Give them a radio. If you get settled and need something, we broadcast on channels eleven and fourteen. We will need to keep the car. Sorry, but good running vehicles like yours will be hard to find over the next few weeks." He lets go of my shoulders and another set grabs me from behind and raises me to my feet. They force us back out of the room and down a hall. The bustle of people working fills the air. We are back in the room where they were unloading their supplies.

Another door opens and I am shoved outside. The warmth sun beats down on the black bag. Bits of sun penetrate the fabric.

"Stop here," a voice commands. The zip tie is cut, and my hands are freed. The bag is ripped from my head. I squint my eyes as they adjust to the sun. My eyes focus. Piles of bodies cover the ground outside the barricades. Two people are on their knees by one of the piles, with black bags over their heads. A man stands behind them and fires two shots into the back of both of their heads. The bodies fall forward onto the pile of the dead. I quickly turn to face the person that has released me. It's the big guy with the toothpick.

"What was that?" I point at the fresh kills.

"Them?" he grunts.

"Yes, them. Why kill them?" I am scared to ask. I don't want it to happen to me, but I don't understand it.

"Were they bit?" asks Sara.

"They had violent criminal backgrounds. That is who Brother Paul was talking about," he shifts the pick from one side to the other.

"What if you're all wrong?" Frank spits.

"Wrong?" Toothpick smirks.

"What if they find a cure? What if this isn't Revelations? You think God wants you killing people?" Frank puffs out his chest.

"It is not up to me. If Brother Paul says kill them, we kill them," Toothpick pokes his finger into Frank's chest.

"You're okay with committing murder?" I ask with full sincerity. It catches Toothpick off guard. I see it in his eyes. He is conflicted.

"God tells Brother Paul who stays and who goes. There is no higher command than God," Toothpick rests his hand on the gun strapped to his body.

"Nothing ridiculous about that," Frank says sarcastically.

"Brother Paul talks directly with The Almighty. God tells him who to trust," Toothpick points back at the church. "Every man, woman and child in there is alive because of Brother Paul. We would do anything for that man. He will see us to the Promise Land," he gives me a wink. Great, I have a neighbor that talks directly with God and has an army of gun wielding followers at his command. I feel safer already.

Another man has our weapons and passes them back to each of us. He sports a short crewcut that makes him look like *Forest Gump*. I slide all of the knives and machetes back onto my belt. He hands me my spear. It feels wonderful in my hands. I missed having it.

"Nice spear," Gump sneers. I look at the rifle hanging off his shoulder.

"I don't have to reload it," I retest the blade to check if it is solid, "How many have you killed?"

Gump gives me a nasty smile. "Plenty and the day has just started."

"What are you going to do if you run out of ammo?" Frank questions.

"We have enough to kill everyone in Vancouver. Twice," Toothpick says proudly. Frank re-straps his shoulder holsters and takes his bag.

"Where's my SKS?" Frank grunts.

"In the bag," Toothpick grunts back.

"Here's the radio. It has a fresh set in it. Do not call us unless you really, really need us," Gump hands it over to me.

"We got our own fucking problems so do not bug us," Toothpick raises his rifle and aims it behind us. He quickly fires a single shot. We spin around. The second my head turns an infected falls to its face. The shot was a hundred yards away and Toothpick nailed it right between the eyes.

"See you around," says Gump as the two of them walk away.

"Holy shit," I say it under my breath. It was remarkable.

We circle up and get ourselves sorted.

"You're bleeding," says Sara as she wipes the tears away from her face.

"I thought so," I drag my hand over my forehead. "I'll be fine. Is everyone okay?" Devon's eyes are drenched with tears. I grab him by his backpack and pull him close to me.

"It's okay?" I say quietly.

"Yeah," he has the snubs.

"What did they do to you?" Sara clears her throat.

"I don't know. They held something cold to my neck. I don't know what it was. I thought a knife. I don't know." he can't look me in the eyes. I give him a little shake with the backpack strap, like I am shaking off the bad vibes.

"Don't worry about it." I tell him, Devon nods his head.

Our powwow is broken up when another round of gunfire pierces our ears. Behind the church is a giant field with trees surrounding the edges. A large pack of infected storm out of the trees and are gunned down immediately.

A car full of people pulls into the back of the church. They get the same greeting we did. It's a lot better being on this side of it. I look back at the tree line and focus on which way to go.

"Take 139th. It is not too bad," Gump yells back at us. I give him a halfhearted wave. I really do not get them. They let us go and give us back all our weapons, but totally screw us by taking our car. We need to get out of here before God changes his mind.

"You guys ready?" I look my crew over. Frank has his SKS locked and loaded. Devon has his spear at the ready. Sara has her machete gripped tight in her hand. "Good. Let's go."

I take a sip of water. I am gassing out so I take another long drag. I take off and jog past the barricade. The cut on my ankle kills with every step. We head for a clearing in the trees. Back on foot. Marvelous.

Chapter 16

One mile. One more goddamn mile of pain before I get home to my family. On a treadmill at the gym I can finish a mile in less than eight minutes. That is if I am fresh, not suffering from a hangover or went too hard on leg day. That is also on a rubber surface and in an air conditioned room. Out here on the hard, hot, deadly streets we will be lucky to get a mile done in a half hour. We creep up slowly to the tree line behind the church and pass by the infected that Toothpick gunned down. The blood soaked letterman's jacket tells me that it is a local high school kid. He is only a few years younger than Devon and Sara. It is quiet on the other side of the trees. I push through a set of evergreens. Ahead of us is a little backyard. There is a dog house, a trampoline and some outdoor kids' toys, but no sign of movement. I take a knee in the grass. The two trees give us a little hiding place to watch from. I turn to face the team.

"Let's keep it quiet. Only shoot if you have to. Stay close," I turn back around and there is an infected sprinting out of the house. I was not ready and I miss it with my spear. I catch it in its shoulder. The force knocks me to my butt. Devon is ready and stabs it right up its nose. I pull out my spear and Frank helps me up to my feet.

I sneak out from the trees and head straight for the side of the house. There is an old beat up truck in the driveway. It blocks the view of the street. Both front tires are flat and it is covered in rust. This hunk of junk has been here a long time. It is a tetanus shot waiting to happen so I steer clear of the busted up grill. We have to squeeze between the house and the truck. It is so close my shoulders grind on the wall and the quarter panel of the Ford. I stop at the edge of the house and give the street a good look. It looks normal. By that I mean there is not a horde of infected looking to tear us apart. There are piles in the street. Good sized piles of human meat. It looks like World War II footage. Behind the scenes of the concentration camps. The worst parts of mankind on film. We can thank Brother Paul for this horrific scene. Must be how Gump knew that 139th was not "too bad."

I take off across the driveway and into the next yard. It has a few large trees and some shrubs to camouflage us. We squat down behind the foliage. I look out to see if the next block is clear. Frank pulls at my sleeve.

"Are we gonna red rover from tree to tree the whole way?" he grumbles. "If I lead the way I can blast down close to sixty of them before I'd have to reload. We sprint hard and go as far as we can. Then find a house to hole up in as I reload and you three keep them off me."

"That sounds good," Sara backs him. I am afraid to get caught out in the open, surrounded with no escape, but I can't wait to get home.

"How's your ankle?" Devon looks down at the dark red bandage wrapped around my ankle.

I nod my head. "It kills, but I think you're right. We need to move fast," I pat Frank on the back. "You lead."

Frank stands up, readjusts his bag, pulls out the magazine on his SKS and checks to make sure it is still full. He snaps it in and pulls back the bolt. He takes off charging down the front yard and out into the street. We follow right behind.

I hang to Frank's left. Devon is on his right. Sara stays behind between Devon and I. We form a flying V. I scan the west side of the street. We roll past house after house and zig-zag past the dead. Brother Paul's teams have been very busy in the few hours since this started. The piles of ex-humans are so foul. Each one has a solid foot of sour goop circled around it. Even out in the open the smell of the sun soaked corpse wreaks havoc on my already suffering nose. I thought I smelled bad. When I was a kid my Dad would make runs to the dump. He would take my brother and me along to help empty the back of his truck. The only part of it I remember is the smell. That almost sweet smell of old junk getting tossed into one immense mountain.

One of the houses on the block has boarded up its doors and windows. A set of eyes watch us from the second story. I am glad to see that not every house has been abandoned. Straight ahead of us is an apartment complex. That is the problem with this area. Tons of people stacked on top of each other, apartment complex after apartment complex. So many people to try and save. So many people to turn into the infected. Frank fires a quick three shot burst. His gun is louder than I thought it would be. He cut down an infected in the intersection. A caravan of cars blast down the street and run right over the fresh kill. The body's crushed into paste. It is a couple of trucks and a sedan. They are filled to the brim with people and supplies.

We enter the intersection quickly and the street to our left is overrun. The infected are headed our way. We pick up the pace. Frank takes down those at the head of the pack.

"Head for the apartment!" I call out. There is a gap between each building. I point for the gap. "That way!" This opening leads us to a parking lot. I look back and the monsters are in hot pursuit. The opening between the buildings forces them to funnel down. They come at us, stumbling over each other. They can only fit three bodies at a time through the breach. Frank sees it too and he opens fire. Some of the shots take down two at a time. It is fantastic to watch him. He is not rushed. He takes his time. He empties his mag quickly and drops fifteen of them.

"Watch our back!" I tell Sara. The stack of bodies slows the rest down and the three of us use our blades to hack and slash them to pieces. Two creatures charge out of the parking lot behind us. Sara chops one of their heads in two like a cantaloupe.

"Guys!" She calls out and Devon whips around and finishes the last one. Frank pops the banana magazine out and flips it around. He has the second magazine, locked and loaded, in a matter of seconds.

"Get back!" Frank growls. We drop back and he opens up on them. The man is a surgeon. He cuts the ranks of this diseased army down by half. The one or two that get passed his kill zone are taken out quickly by one of the three of us. The heap of bodies stands four feet tall. His SKS clicks empty. The last couple of stragglers climb over the hill of bodies. Our three blades finish them off. As soon as I can, I have to make Sara a spear. She gets so close with the machete that it sprays her with blood. Every other kill splatters her with sticky goo. If I could figure out a way to bolt a machete to a walking stick, that would be a killer weapon. Frank has his SKS slung back on his shoulder and both Berettas out. He caps the last two.

"Wow!" Devon jumps with excitement.

"I need to reload," Frank holsters one of the guns.

"I need to wash off," Sara wipes her face. I look over the parking lot. Most of the spots are empty. There should be a lot of empty apartments to choose from.

I run diagonally across the lot. We head for an apartment on the west side of the complex. I spot a door that looks good. No car out front. No blood on the window. It is a first floor unit. These apartments are built into the ground so the first floor is more of a day light basement.

I get face to face with the door, give it a tap, press my ear to the wood and listen for any movement. I tap it a little harder. I shrug my shoulders back to the group.

"I think it's empty."

"Let's give it a try," Sara gets her machete up and ready. I step back from the door.

"I've always wanted to do this," I throw a brutal front kick. One of the best legged kicks I have ever thrown. My foot makes contact with the door and I am stopped cold. I nailed it but the door won this round. My left knee takes most of the punishment. "Shit," I grab my knee.

"I thought that would have like, worked," Devon is disappointed. Frank steps up and blasts the knob with his gun. The door swings open.

"You loosened it for me," Frank jokes as he enters the apartment.

The place smells of stale cigarette smoke. There is a lot of clutter around the front door and all of the lights are out. I turn the bolt lock and put on the chain on.

"Hello?" Devon calls.

"Gunshot would have alerted them. No one's here," Sara walks over to the kitchen sink and turns on the faucet. She finds a washcloth and goes to work cleaning herself. The place is messy but it does not look like someone was packing to leave.

"Let's hurry," Frank drops his bag down onto the kitchen table and unzips it. He pops the mag out of the SKS and pulls out a box of ammo. He quickly goes to work filling them. Propped up in the corner by the front door is a Louisville Slugger.

"Devon, give Sara the sheath to the machete," I grab up the bat and take it into the kitchen. I pull open the drawers around the sink and find the knife drawer. I find a set of long and sturdy cooking knives. They are thick in the spine and have a full tang blade. I search the cupboards until I find a roll of Duct Tape. I use half the roll of tape, but I put both blades at the head of the bat. I test it to make sure they are sturdy. I swing it into the back of a chair at the kitchen table. It snaps right through the back of the chair and the blades hold firm. I hand the bat to Sara.

"That should give you a little more distance."

She takes it and gives it a swing, "Thanks."

I take a long drag of water. The bladder goes empty. I need to refill my water. I pull off my backpack and pop it open. I pull out a couple bags of jerky and a Snickers bar. I toss a bag of jerky to Devon. I tear into my Snickers. I am going to have to find a big box of these at a store before they are all gone. I know that most grocery stores have only what is on the shelf and when it is gone, it is gone. I pull out the water bladder of my pack and it hits me I have to take a piss.

"We should use the bathroom," I put down my bag and spear.

I head to the back of the apartment looking for the bathroom. Two doors are open and they are the bedrooms, but the third door is shut. I open the door and smell it. Death. I have it only open a few inches when the set of teeth smashes into the door frame.

"Shit!" I gasp. It is a woman in her thirties. She has turned. Her fingers are wrapped around the edge of the door. I quickly grab the knob with both hands to keep it from swinging open. Her hands are covered in blood and she fights like a wild animal to get out of the bathroom.

"Guys!" I call them. Devon is first to show up.

"Whoa!" he blurts out.

"Get her!" I tell him. He pulls his knife and steps up to the door. He stabs down into her skull and the body drops. I push hard on the door to get it to move her body. I get the door open and I back away from the bathroom. My hand automatically goes up to my mouth.

"Oh no," Devon whispers. Sara and Frank have joined us and they see the horror that is this bathroom.

"What?" Sara whimpers.

"Mother of God!" Frank says in disgust. Every inch of the bathroom looks like it is covered in blood. On the mirror are the words "I'm sorry". The message is written in blood.

In the bathtub are two small children. Their heads have been crushed in by the lid off the back of a toilet. There is a razor blade on the counter. It is soaked in blood. I look back at the woman's body and there are deep red slits across both wrists.

I am going to lose it. The thought of my wife doing this is enough to send me to the nuthouse.

"I'm almost loaded," Frank turns away and heads back to the kitchen. I pull the door closed.

Back in the kitchen I dig under the kitchen sink. There has to be a bucket around here somewhere.

"Go in the sink," Frank clicks the last few rounds into the banana magazine.

"I can't piss in a sink," Anger builds. I can feel it. My face is flush. I am hungry, dehydrated and every part of my body aches. I smash around the contents of the cabinet.

"Piss in the sink," he says again.

"Fuck off." I have never ever told someone to "fuck off." I can't believe I said it. Frank drops his gun on the table. I quickly turn and he has got a hold of my collar. His face is inches from mine. I am pinned up against the sink.

"Are you angry?"

"Let go of me!" I push him back.

"Are you pissed off?" he pushes against me even harder.

"Guys," Sara grabs us both by our shoulders. She pushes and pulls to separate us.

"You think your wife's dead? And your kids? They're all gone. Eaten by some monster and you didn't save them." Frank's words cut me to my soul.

"Shut up!" I slam my forearm against his and break his hold on my collar. Then I push him back and throw a right cross. My fist mangles his lips. I am such an idiot. Why risk breaking my hand? Why punch this man who has done everything to try to help me get home? Frank falls back against the kitchen table. My hand kills but I did not break it. I know I hurt him, but he is not showing any pain. Frank rubs his mouth and spits out a glob of blood on the floor.

"Feel better?" he goes back to loading the magazine.

"No, I don't. I shouldn't have hit you. I'm sorry."

"That love tap? Don't worry about it," he smiles back at me and tosses his bag up onto his shoulder.

"Your wife's going to be fine. I know it," Devon chimes in from the living room. Bits of jerky fall from his mouth as he talks. I turn my back to him and I piss in the sink. I know Sara is only feet from me, but I have to go so badly. She does not seem to care. She didn't even turn away.

"How do you know?" I have to talk louder over the noise from the sink.

"You told her to stay in the bedroom, get the gun and don't let anyone know she's there," he pours the last of the bag into his mouth and tosses the empty plastic to the floor. I finish pissing in the sink and rinse it out as I wash my hands. I fill the bladder for my pack. "Look around. Like, they aren't beating down this lady's door to get in here. She could've been fine and I don't see a husband in any of the pictures. She didn't have anyone coming home like Karen does. It was her and the kids and she lost hope. She lost it fast," Devon smiles brightly at me, his lip is swollen, but he still manages a smile to make me feel better.

I finish filling my water bladder. I face my friends. "You're right," I reconnect the bladder to my pack.

"You boys okay now?" Sara pats me on the shoulder. Frank and I nod. I sling my bag onto my back and snap it secure. Frank is ready. Sara slides her machete into the sheath on her hip and picks up her new blade bat. Devon and I grab our spears and head for the door.

I look out the peephole. "There's two out there," I whisper. Frank is right behind me. "Let Devon and I take those two. Then we head north." Frank and Devon switch spots behind me. I unlock the bolt and swing the door open. The two monsters do not know what hit them. We are out the door with spears jammed in the back of their heads in under two seconds. We take the same triangle position as before with Frank in the lead. The four of us sprint hard across the lot. A car sits ahead of us, its front windows smashed in. The driver and his passenger have turned. They are strapped into the front seats and their arms claw out the window at us. They were bitten on their arms and hands. Both are missing most of their fingers and the bones of their forearms are exposed.

"We should put them down. If they get out they could hurt someone," Sara readies her weapon.

"She's right. We should put down every one of them we come across," Frank leads us over to the car.

"I'll take the passenger," I split off from the group to the passenger side. I get my spear up and ready to stab. I know this person. She works at the local Trader Joe's. I put her out of her misery. Sara uses the blade bat and it destroys the man's face.

We regroup and head for another gap between the last buildings on this lot. When we get to the edge of the building we pause for a moment. Ahead of us is a major intersection. From here I can see my apartment complex. My heart skips a beat. The intersection is an absolute mess. It is filled with cars. Some have flipped over on their sides, a few are on fire and a couple are just burnt out shells. There are black skeletons seared to the car seats and they move like bad animatronic robots. The tight skin and loss of muscle control give the bodies a herky jerky movement. There is a good sized horde around the intersection. I glance over to the right and there's a church. As far as I can tell there is only a couple to get through if we head for the church. We dart across this little chunk of grass. It is covered in trees and scrubs. The plants keep us hidden from the infected. There is a fence that separates this apartment complex from the street. We follow the fence to the edge of the property.

I peek around the fence and the street is clear. Dead ahead of us is a minivan that is flipped over and resting on its roof. The van is laid out across two lanes. We stay low and sprint across the sidewalk and hide behind the van. I pause for a second to catch my breath. In the next lane is a U-haul truck. That is the next spot to get to, but there is a fifteen foot chunk of concrete to cross where we will have nothing to hide behind. A set of infected hands reach out from the overturned van. They grab Frank's leg. He screams in shock. I drop down to the ground and come face to face with a young girl. Thirteen maybe, and beside the bite marks on her hand she looks totally fine.

"Oh God, she's a kid," I look up at the others. Frank pulls his leg out of her hands.

"They've heard us!" Sara taps me on the back.

"Kill it man!" Devon is ready to move. I know she is a vicious killer now, but hours ago she was someone's little girl. I jab my spear into its face. A little piece of me dies every damn time I have to do this. Like most American males I was born and raised on violent movies. Over the years I have heard groups complain that it desensitizes kids to violence, and maybe it does. Right now, I am glad I watched those movies. I am glad I am slightly desensitized. If I was any more sensitive to the kinds of horrible acts I have had to commit today, I would be a blob of jelly curled up on the ground. We cross into the empty parking lot and make for the front doors. This church was not as prepared for the end, as Brother Paul's. It is a ghost town.

We hit the doors and they are locked. Frank lets off a round and the glass pours to the ground. We enter quickly into the large foyer. To our right is where mass is held. In front of us is a door. I pull up on the handle and it opens up to a large Sunday school room. We scramble in and slam the door behind us. I lock the doorknob. Sara already has a chair dragged over to the door. We quietly slide the back of the chair up under the knob. We hear the crackling sound of broken glass underfoot on the other side of the door. They have lost track of us. There is another door across the classroom. Frank has his ear up against it. We tiptoe across the room. Frank slowly opens the door and it is another entryway. There is the same kind of glass doors that lead to the outside. This place has two main entrances. They must have really packed them in here on Sundays. To our right is the place of worship. A few of our dead friends have found their way into the room. They take off, tripping over the pews the second they see us.

There is a large set of double doors pinned open to this room. Frank grabs one of the doors. I take the other door. I kick up the stopper and push the door closed. We slam them shut right in the face of a dead cop. His heavy body crashes into the door and it pops back open. Devon mashes his body up against the door and it slams back shut.

"Why didn't you shoot it?" I ask Frank.

He furrows his brow at me, "It's a church!" That was not the response I was expecting.

"Find something to jam into the handles!" I call to Sara. Body after body hits the other side of the door. She scans the room and it is practically empty. Against the far wall is a hip high table with some bibles on it. She grabs the table and drags it over to us. Bibles fall as it shimmies across the carpet. She tips the table over and the rest of the bibles fall. If one more body hits this door it is going to open. She gets the end of the table up and slides one of the legs through the two handles. The back corner of the table anchors into the carpet, the front corner jams into the door. I do not feel any pressure from the monsters on the other side. It worked! I grab the leg and give it a good pull. The aluminum bends and it locks the leg into the door handles. We race for the exit. The door pops open and we run. Frank guns down two in the north parking lot of the church.

We sprint across the parking lot and head for 136th. On the other side of this street is a park, baseball and football fields. It is one large chunk of grass that surrounds a middle school. We come to a stop once we hit the grass.

"My God." Devon's voice cracks.

"We can't…it's too many…kids," Sara stutters. This all started around one o'clock and school was in session. They must have tried to evacuate the kids. There are two buses out front of the school and they are smeared with blood. Most of the little ones are around the front of the school. There are a hundred pint sized bloody bodies and at least twenty faculty members blocking our way. It is by far the most heartbreaking, horrific sight we have come across today.

"Should we go around?" Devon groans.

"If we go around we might run into even more and they could all be full sized. We have to go straight through," Frank pops out his magazine and reloads the couple of shots he fired.

"We can't do that. They're kids!" Sara turns her back to them.

"My place is right there," I point. "My family is waiting for me."

"We should go around," Devon pleads.

"They're not human anymore. They're killers like the rest of them," Frank pops his magazine back in.

"Frank's right. There's too many. We can't leave them this close to my place. Oh, I can't believe I'm gonna say this," I drop my head. "It shouldn't be as hard. We're faster, stronger and have a better reach than most of them."

Sara can't believe I said it either, "Come on," she stabs her blade bat into the turf.

"If we do this we all have to agree. I don't want to get bit because someone went soft," Frank turns to face us.

"Devon, I need your help for a little longer. We are so close," I grab his arm and give it a tug.

"Fine," he shakes his head.

"Sara, are you good?" Frank reaches out and gently spins her back around. She nervously jumps up and down on her toes. Like a fighter going into the ring.

"Fuck it. Let's go," she raises her blade bat, ready to kill.

"What's the plan?" Frank spits his gum onto the grass.

"Move fast. Don't get bit. Kill them all," I speak the truth. Frank looks at me from the corner of his eye.

"Great plan," Frank takes the lead. We move quickly across the park and into the baseball field. Frank guns down a couple out in the field.

They hear the gunshots and head our way. Their hero and princess backpacks flop around as they run. It is a parent's greatest fear.

There is a covered basketball court that is connected to the school's gym. The lights are still on in the building. I take a good look at the gym doors. They are steel and glass and the glass has wire mesh built into it. It gives me an idea.

"This way!" I run for the gym. Frank has gunned down another fifteen.

We get to the basketball court and Frank's shots echo even louder with a roof overhead. I slam up against the door and look around inside.

"What are we doing?!" Sara yells. The gym is empty. I pull on the door and it opens.

"Get inside!" I tell them. Devon is first, followed by Sara. Frank empties his magazine into the leaders. I grab him by his shoulder strap and pull him into the building. The door shuts behind us.

"Hold the other door," I hold on tight to the handle. Devon and Sara grab and hold the other door. Seconds later the little bodies and a few of the big ones crash into the gym doors. Frank flips around his magazine and he is ready to go. It does not take long and there is thirty plus crammed up against the doors. Their own bodies have locked the doors and now they can't get in.

"Alright Frank."

"What?"

I point out the window, "This glass isn't bullet proof." I step away from the door. He slowly walks up to the window and raises his gun. Little fingers claw at the window. He is slow to pull the trigger. The muzzle of his gun is right next to the glass. He opens fire and his rounds rip a hole through the window. It doesn't take him long to get through his magazine. When he is done there are still a lot of them out there but the hole in the glass is large enough I can fit my spear through it. I pat Frank on his shoulder. He steps to the side and I raise my spear up to the hole. Frank walks over to a wall, backs up to it and slides down to his butt. I make sure the lanyard is wrapped around my wrist, take aim and quickly take down the stragglers. The bodies pile up by the door with each strike of my spear. I have taken down ten before I feel the tears stream down my face. There are more than twenty left out there. They stumble and trip over their fallen classmates and students. There are so many bodies they can't get close enough to the door for my spear to reach them. Frank unzips his bag and pulls out another box of ammo. He reloads slowly.

"Let's take five," Devon says as he gets down next to Frank. I wipe my eyes on my sleeve. There is a lone basketball on the floor of the gym.

"Wanna shoot hoops?" I ask. I get a few chuckles out of them. The kind of laughs you get when someone says something funny but very inappropriate. I feel a madness growing inside. In a handful of hours I have seen so much destruction that I feel changed. I could take a hundred showers and never feel clean.

"Let's see if we can make it through the school and pop out a door close to the apartment." I take a sip of water.

"What about the rest of them?" Sara has a new nail in her mouth and she works it to the quick. There is a noise at the window. One of them made it up to the door. It reaches through the window.

"There's only a couple left. We'll deal with them out there."

"Almost done," Frank flips the magazines over and works on the last one.

I jog over to door on the far wall and press my ear to it. A few good taps against it and I do not hear anything. I pop the door open and look around. It is a hallway. The lights are out but it is clear.

"You guys ready?" Frank pops his mag back into the rifle. I prop the door open in case we have to run back this way.

The hallways are lined with papier-mâché projects and colorful construction paper, flowers and trees mostly. Their names scribbled down on the works of art. Ashley, Kristin, Zack, Gunner, Heather, so many little boys and girls that never had a chance. We pass a series of classrooms and get to a wide, empty hall. It is the main entrance into the school. The outside glass doors are spattered in blood. There are still a handful of them out by the buses.

"Look," Devon points outside. The inside of the buses are what caught his eye. Little hands paw at the windows. Both buses are full. Every seat has a dead child in it. I try the next door to let us into the backend of the school. It is locked.

"Crap. We'll have to go this way," I point at the main doors. "We'll take down the ones right outside and head for the apartment."

"Yeah," Frank agrees. I push open the first of two doors that go outside.

"Save your ammo. We can take them." I push open the last door. The door clicks and screeches, it lets them know exactly where we are. They charge straight for us and the three of us hammer the little infected and remaining staff. Frank hangs back to make sure we do not get surrounded. We are down to the last couple infected. A few more swings and this is over.

BOOM!

The gunshot did not come from Frank. Devon is on the ground. Blood seeps from his leg. The shot came from a man on the other side of the parking lot with a large revolver in his hand. He is covered in blood.

"Stop killing them!" the man pleads. Frank has his gun up and trained on the man's chest.

"We have to! If they bite you you'll turn!" I yell back at him as I move to Devon's side. Sara takes down the last infected child. The man runs across the parking lot and aims at Sara.

BOOM!

He misses.

"Hold your fire!" I put pressure on Devon's leg.

"They're dead!" Sara yells as she ducks down.

"My baby's here. Don't kill them!" his voice cracks. Tears and snot run down his face. He has lost his shit. I lift up Devon's leg the round passed through. Everything I know about gunshot wounds I learned from TV and movies. I can't tell if it is better that it passed through or not. He has two holes in his leg but at least I will not have to dig around for the bullet. The man looks up at a bus and he falls to his knees.

"Oh, God no!" he found who he was looking for.

"AM I GONNA DIE?!" Devon grabs me.

"No, you're not! You're gonna go into shock, but you won't die! I promise."

The man is on the ground, screaming at the top of his lungs.

"What should we do?" Frank keeps his gun aimed at the man.

He gets up from the asphalt and heads for the back of the bus. "Teagan!" he grabs the release lever on the emergency door and pulls it down.

"What are you doing?!" I look up from Devon.

"My baby!" he swings the door open and they pour out onto him. Frank fires and downs a couple but it is too late. They have him. Their little mouths and hands tear into his flesh. Frank fires off a few more rounds and then his gun stops firing.

"It's jammed," Frank works the bolt on the SKS, but it is not clearing the casing. The bus is packed with kids and they tumble through the rear emergency exit. There must be forty blood thirsty infected kids. The man is smothered in bodies. His screams become thick gargles as the infected tear out his throat. The rest of them have set their sights on us. Frank works at his gun. Sara pulls on my backpack for us to leave. Devon tries to keep me close and I do not know what to do. I can't leave Devon. I won't leave him. I can see my actual apartment. H7. Is right there. So Goddamn close.

Chapter 17

Frank lets go of his SKS and the shoulder strap swings it back under his arm. He pulls both Berettas out and takes down the first bunch of infected. More and more dead children fall from the back of the bus. They land hard on the ground. Some of them break their limbs as they fall. Their little forearms bend backwards as they tumble to the ground. I grab Devon's wrists and pull him to his feet. He makes a hell of a lot of racket as I move him. He dances around on his good leg until I get my shoulder down in his mid section and toss him up into a fireman's carry. Thank God he is skinny.

"Grab his spear!" I bark at Sara. She clobbers an infected ten year old with her blade bat and then grabs the spear.

We race. The final sprint home. After hours of running scared I will finally be home. We are minutes from walking through my front door. There is a field of grass that separates the school from my apartment complex and a fence separates the two. No way I can climb it with Devon so we have to run to the end. Of course the end of the fence sits at the far corner of the field. It is three football fields long. I need a break. An hour or two on my couch would feel great. To rest, breathe easy and try to forget today. If I sit down, I will not get back up. I will fall asleep. I can't wait to hold my girls. All three of them. If it was possible I would never let them go. I love to hold them in my arms and feel the skin of their cheeks against my neck. Their little hands wrapped around my fingers. When I see my wife I am going to give her a good long kiss. Usually when I get home from work we give each other a peck to say hello. This time I am going in for a long one. Maybe try and turn it French. I know I am filthy and stink to high heaven, but I bet I can make it happen. I think she loves me enough to kiss this filth.

Devon is heavy on my shoulder and he throws off how I run. Instead of being light and running on the balls of my feet, I run flatfooted and my joints scream in pain. Devon's gunshot wound pours blood. The back of his green camo pants has turned dark purple. If he bleeds out and dies while he is on my shoulder he might try and bite me. With every step my anxiety builds. My brain plays out awful scenarios over and over again. I am too late. They are not there waiting for me. Something terrible has happened. All these thoughts are repeated over and over again. Plus, the horde of hungry infected preteens does not help. They chase after us like it is a game. The most horrifying game of tag ever. I look back as I cross from the parking lot to the field. Sara is behind me. Frank is not far behind her. He holsters one of his Berettas so he can change out the magazine as he runs. He gets both mags changed out for fresh ones and whips around and opens fire. He takes down another ten. His aim is off. He got the horde of kids down to about thirty. It is still too many to fight out in the open. They will surround us and we will be goners. We are halfway across the field.

There is a gate in the fence at the corner of the field. It is unlocked and wide open. Frank has caught back up with me.

"Sara, get the gate!" It takes everything I have to get the words out of my mouth. Devon's weight on my shoulder crushes my lungs. She takes off and in a matter of seconds she is way ahead of us.

She gets through the gate and drops her weapons. It is rusty so she works it back and forth until she is able to get it to shut. Frank gets there first and I am right behind him. As soon as we are clear she has the gate shut and lever down, locking it. I lay Devon down on a patch of grass. His face has gone white. His eyelids flutter.

"Don't go to sleep!" I give him a little punch in the arm. The infected are at the fence, but they can't get over it.

"Okay." Devon nods at me.

"I need a knife," Frank gasps. I pull one from my hip and hand it to him. I pull my belt off and wrap it around Devon's leg. My extra knives and machete fall to the ground. I get the belt tight around his leg.

"Get the medkit out of my pack."

Sara steps behind me and unzips the pack. She finds it, pops it open and finds a couple large bandages and some gauze. We get bandages on both wounds and wrap it as tight as we can. I use my belt to hold everything in place.

"There we go!" Frank has worked out the jammed casing. He slides the bolt back and forth and his rifle is ready to rock. He empties the last of his magazine into the monsters on the other side of the fence. Frank flips the banana mag around and takes care of the rest.

"Come on buddy. You're doing good. We're almost there. Take a drink of water," I help him get his water line into his mouth.

"Can you toss the knives and machetes into my pack with the medkit?" I ask Sara. She tucks it and the knives into the bag. Frank picks up the machete and slides it onto his belt.

"I'm tapped out and need to reload everything," Frank swings the SKS onto his back and picks up Devon's spear. I take a look around the parking lot. My wife's green PT Cruiser is in her spot.

"Jim!" Frank needs my attention. I look up and it is another nightmare. We go from the very young to the very old. The thing I feared earlier today. There is an old folks home on the next block and it looks like every single one of them has been turned and found this apartment complex. The one good thing about super old infected people is that they are slow. Imagine an old person, someone in their late eighties walking around. It takes them forever to get anywhere. Then add being dead and chewed on, and you got a group of deadly snails blocking us from my apartment. These poor old people are horrible to look at. Open robes and nothing on underneath. It is amazing how many of them have colostomy bags. It is a cruel prank Mother Nature plays on us. Seventy plus years with a normal functioning body and then everything falls apart the last two decades.

I pull Devon to his feet. Frank has his revolver and he puts down the first six old people.

"H7! Come on!" I wrap Devon's arm over my shoulders and he hops along on his good leg. Frank and Sara lead the way. The two of them make a path. They decimate the retired old folks. I drag Devon. His eyes are shut.

"Don't go to sleep! Wake your ass up and help me!" He pops his peeper's open and tries to help carry more of his weight on his good leg. We get to the sidewalk outside my home.

"You gotta hop up!" Devon hops up onto the curb.

Each building is made up of four apartments. There are two on the top floor and two on the main. My place is on the first floor. The door is tucked back into the building. A flight of stairs to the second story takes up half of the entryway. At the top of the stairs someone has blocked up the landing with two by fours and plywood. I have lived here almost two years and I barely know my neighbors. There is a deaf guy across from us. A deaf neighbor is great because he does not make any noise. Above us is a young pothead couple. At almost the same time every night we will hear them cough like crazy on their back porch. Then the smell of weed creeps down to our place. Kitty corner from us is a young family like mine. Husband, wife and three kids. I can never remember their names, but I think he works in construction. He must have built the blockage at the top of the stairs. There is a group of bodies outside my door.

I don't recognize any of them. There are a few old people mixed in with a few men in their late forties. I get to my front door and there are several bullet holes right below the peephole. They were fired from the inside. Something else I know from TV. Shotgun blasts are peppered across the wall next to my front door. Someone gunned down the dead bodies. The door to my neighbor's is wide open. Blood covers the door, carpet and hallway leading into his place. My deaf neighbor's body lies on the floor. It is torn in half. His torso lies in the hallway. He has turned. Once he sees me he drags himself toward the front door. His intestines pull tight and the bottom half of his body pulls around the corner into the hallway. He drags his legs behind him. Sara and Frank take down the infected close to the entry, but there are too many out there. Soon they will overwhelm us. I kick at the front door.

"Karen! Open up!" I kick it a few more times. "KAREN! KAREN!" my voice is hoarse with panic.

"HURRY UP! THERE'S TOO MANY!" Sara and Frank back up from the infected. We need to get inside right now. The deaf neighbor pulls himself through his doorway. He is an ankle biter. His hands slip in the blood that coats the entryway. One of his feet gets caught on the corner of the hallway. As he pulls himself though the doorway his intestines unspool from his torso.

"KAREN!" I give it one last kick. Nothing. I am going to lose my mind! When my kids were first born I would call home to tell Karen I was on my way. About two out of ten times I would call and she would not answer. I would call over and over and still no answer. My mind would go crazy with different horrible scenarios. Mostly that she was dead and the kids are now missing. I would get home and she would be fine. The kids were fine. They would be playing or sleeping like kids do. Her phone would be on vibrate so she could get the kids to sleep without worrying about it going off and waking them up. I would get myself all worked up over nothing.

I prop Devon up against the wall and dig into my pocket. I get my keys out. My deaf neighbor's hands claw at my legs. I kick them away. It feels like a classic horror movie. The killer creeps slowly towards his victim as the young beautiful virgin fumbles with the keys. I stomp down onto the head of the infected. Its teeth crunch into the concrete. I didn't kill it. I only gave it a disgusting jagged smile. Its top teeth have snapped in half. It still tries to grab my legs. I get the right key and the door pops open. I grab Devon and push him in.

"COME ON!" I call to the others. I whip around and slash at the infected on the ground. My spear finishes the job and my poor, deaf neighbor is put to rest. Frank and Sara follow me into my place and I slam the door shut, lock it.

I drop my spear and push passed my guests to get to my bedroom. Frank and Sara help Devon to the couch.

"KAREN? KIDS? VALERIE? ROBIN?" the bedroom door is open, but nobody is there. Our laptop is on the bed. A video game prompts me to click continue. I check the closet. Nothing. The case to my handgun is open and the gun is gone. I look over the rest of the closet and Karen's boots are gone along with some of her clothes. I know they are not under the bed. We use an old queen box as a bed frame so we do not have to worry about someone hiding under there. I leave the bedroom and check the computer room. It is a junk room really. My hands shake. They are not there. There is another dead body I do not recognize on the floor. A large puddle of blood surrounds its head. I move back down the hall. They are not in the bathroom. I get to the living room and see that my sliding glass door is broken. Glass covers the floor and there is blood everywhere. A dead body lies outside on the back porch. Inside is another mound of bodies. They sit by the sliding glass door. All senior citizens. Someone has blasted this door and these bodies to pieces with a shotgun. There are empty shells all over the floor. There are also shells from my Ruger everywhere. Bullet holes pock the sheetrock in the kid's playroom. My family is not here! I fall to my knees, sobbing. I failed. Everything I did was not enough. All the horrible things I had to go through added up to nothing. No. No. I didn't make it home in time. I can't see. My eyes are blurred with tears.

"Jim?" Sara calls to me. I look up. At the doorway to the back of my place stands an infected. It comes right on in. Its flesh stripped arms reach out for me. It is an old man in a tracksuit, with big bushy eyebrows. It has a bad tattoo of an anchor on its forearm. He must have been in the Navy. I jump to my feet and grab him. My blood boils. I lift the infected body up into the air and sweep out its legs. We crash to the floor. Its teeth snap inches from my face. I sit up and straddle it. With every fiber of muscle I have left I eviscerate its face with my elbows. I use the shin guards on my forearms to absolutely destroy it. I hear myself screaming but I can't stop. Between blows I catch glimpses of the photos that hang on the walls of this shitty apartment. My family. My little girls. My wedding day. Frank pulls me off the dead body. I kick at it as I get to my feet.

"CALM DOWN!" It is his turn to talk me down off the ledge. He turns me away from the dead thing on the floor. "That won't bring them back." Its head is a two-foot smear on the floor. Some of its blood has splattered onto an Ernie doll that was left on the floor. I got it for Valerie on her first birthday.

She loves that doll and has slept with it more than any other toy.

"We can't stay here," Sara helps Devon back to his feet.

"Where can we go?" Frank lets me go.

"I don't know! My only goal was to get here!" snot runs down my nose and falls off my upper lip. I can't take my eyes off the bloody Ernie. I have got to clean him. Valerie would cry if she saw him like this. I can't function. I have lost myself.

"Go! Go without me! I quit," I zone out and stare at the floor. I can't look anywhere without seeing something that will make me lose it.

"You don't get to quit!" Sara pulls my backpack around so I have to face her. "Maybe they left," she steadies Devon.

"How? The car's still out there!" I can't look her in the eyes.

"We need to go!" Frank grabs my spear and hands it to me.

"I'm not leaving! I can't leave without my family!" I pull my prized high definition plasma TV down off of its stand. It is pulverized when it hits the floor. Frank slaps me across the face. My Krav skills have failed me again. He didn't do it fast, but I couldn't stop him.

"My family is gone! I am still standing! You will stand too. You don't have a choice," Frank's eyes breathe fire at me.

"My family is dead too!" Sara looks at me like I am a selfish child.

"Hey!" There is a voice from outside. Frank pulls out his revolver and quickly reloads it. I step closer to the door and out onto the little chunk of concrete we call the backyard.

"Hello?" I call out.

"Up here," the voice comes from above me. I look up. It is the family that lives kitty corner from us.

"Climb up," the guy says. I wish I could remember his name. I know he has told me it like three times.

"What?" I step a little further onto the grass. He rolls down an emergency rope ladder. It drops down and the bottom rung touches the freshly clipped lawn.

"Come on!"

"Have you seen my family?" I beg. Please, please, please, a glimmer of hope ignites.

"Yeah. They left with a guy in a red truck. About an hour ago." My brother-in-law, Troy, drives a red truck. The flame of hope flickers brighter.

"Did he have a beard?"

"Yeah. Now, come on."

My eyes clear up. My heart lifts. Maybe they are not dead. I have got to regroup and regain focus.

"I have to grab some stuff." I step back into my place.

"You'd better hurry. They're coming!" he yells after me.

"He's got a ladder up to his place," I head straight for the Ernie doll. I grab it and look around for the Bert I got Robin on her first birthday.

"Can we trust them?" Sara moves Devon towards the door.

"Yeah. I guess. I don't really know him, but he's got a family and he always seemed nice," I dig through a pile of toys.

"My names Cliff, again," Cliff calls down to us.

"What about Devon?" Frank puts his revolver away.

I find the other doll and pick it up. I let myself hold them tight for a second. "We'll lift him. Please put this in my bag." I hand the toys to Frank and turn my back to him. He unzips it and forces them in. There is not much room left. I step into my bathroom and open the cabinet under the sink. There is one of those ten-dollar medical kits and a bottle of hydrogen peroxide. I take both. In the hallway closet is another backpack I have had since college. I throw the medical stuff in it. I run back to my bedroom and find my Maglite, and a change of underwear and socks. In the junk room on the bookshelf I grab a book my Mom got me when I joined the Boy Scout's. The book is a field guild to survive outdoors. I cram it into the bag. I look at the dead body on the floor of the room and I notice it was killed with a knife. It sticks out of the side of its skull. I recognize the handle. It is a knife Karen got from her Dad when she was a kid. I pull it out of the dead man's head and wipe the blood off the blade. I put it in my pocket. The last thing I grab is my Dad's old leather jacket. It is a heavy-duty jacket that he wore when he was a young man and rode motorcycles. It has sentimental value. Plus it looks badass. The bag is almost full. Back in the kitchen I pull cans of food down out of the cupboards and fill the bag the rest of the way. On the counter I see a note. It is my wife's handwriting. "WENT TO MOM'S" is all it says. Her brother took her home to her Mom's house. He is a big strong guy and my mother-in-law has a tall fence around her house. If they made it, they could be safe. My mother-in-law, Penny, stockpiles food. She is a food hoarder. It is a good place to hold up. I have to make it there.

I get outside and Sara is already up the ladder. Frank goes next. I toss the backpack up onto the porch and hand up my spear. Cliff already has Devon's spear. Frank gets to the top and they pull him over the rail.

"Alright, you hold the ladder. When I get to the top I'll pull you up. Okay."

Devon's skin is pale and he has dark circles under his eyes. Somehow we have to get him some blood and medication to stop any infection. I start to climb. It is not that high, so I get to the top fast. The group helps me over the rail. I look back and Devon is barely holding on to the ladder. From around the corner of the apartment the old person horde has found us.

"Devon! DEVON!" I call down to him. Finally he looks up. "Step onto the ladder and hold tight."

He tries to put his hurt leg up on to the first rung and screams out in pain. The noise excites the infected.

"Devon! Come on!" Sara begs. He fights to pull himself up fully onto the ladder. The infected are ten feet from him.

"Pull yourself up boy!" Frank slaps at the rail. He tries again and screams at the top of his lungs but he gets both feet up onto the ladder. The monsters are so close. Frank grabs one rope and I take the other. We pull at the same time. When we get a rung up and over the rail I pin it down with my body. The infected reach out. Their fingers brush Devon's legs. He panics and spins around on the ladder. I am about to lose my grip. If they get a hold of the ladder they will pull him right down.

"Pull me up! Pull me up!" Devon cries out. Sara joins us and helps pull on one of the rungs. We get him above their reach. One more rung and I grasp his hands. The three of us pull him over the rail. We all fall to the floor of Cliff's porch. We can't help ourselves, we cry. The four of us lay out on that concrete porch.

"You've been shot," Cliff opens his sliding glass door. "Tina, someone has been shot," Cliff steps into his apartment. We get out from under Devon and I notice six eyes on us. It is Cliff's little girls. Tina enters the living room.

"Girls! Get away from the door," she has only a touch of an accent. She is originally from Mexico. The girls take off and run back to their bedroom.

Cliff has a yoga mat out and on the floor, "Here, lay him on this."

We drag Devon in and lay him down onto the mat. Tina goes to Devon's side and opens his eyes. She looks at his pupils and then holds two fingers to his neck. After a few seconds of counting, she pulls back our bandage job and takes a look at his wounds. Sara kneels down on Devon's other side.

"Do you know what to do?" Sara takes Devon's hand.

"I am working on my second year of nursing school. I know enough to be dangerous," she winks at Devon.

"What a crazy day. It got biblical out there. You want a beer? Hi, I am Cliff and this is Tina." Cliff holds out his hand for Frank.

"Frank," he shakes Cliff's hand, "This is Sara and Devon," he points at them, "Yes, on the beer, please," Frank lets go of his hand

and finds a place to put his bag down. He goes to work right away at reloading his guns.

Cliff heads into the kitchen. My eyes follow him and there are four cases of beer in there.

"You made it to the store?" I ask.

"We were at the store when shit started going down."

"When Karen, my wife, left was…"

He cuts me off. "Yeah, they are all fine. Kids, wife, they looked good. Some guy showed up in a truck with a shotgun. He took out some of the…what did you call them, honey?"

"Zombies," Tina says without looking up from Devon's leg. Cliff is back from the kitchen.

"Zombies, that's right. Yeah, he gunned down a bunch and they took off," Cliff checks out my wounds and bandages, "You look like you have been through hell," he has three beers in his hand. I don't recognize the brand. Some kind of Mexican beer. He hands one to both of us.

"Yeah. It has been a day," I pop open the beer and drain it in one long swallow. Best beer I have ever had.

The End

If you enjoyed this book check out *The Infected: Karen's First Day (Book Two)* and *The Infected: Day Two (Book Three)*.

Coming soon. *Sweet Home.* A story of a small mountain town in Oregon that is visited by a few homicidal maniacs one New Years Eve. Only the strongest in town will survive the night. Expect this book sometime winter of 2015.

Made in the USA
Charleston, SC
03 October 2016